BAD WOLF

SHIFTERS UNBOUND

JENNIFER ASHLEY

JA / AG PUBLISHING

CHAPTER ONE

Broderick McNaughton woke with a raging headache, dry mouth, and what felt like hot bands around his wrists. *What the fuck?*

He didn't remember getting this drunk. He remembered hanging out at Liam's bar for a while then heading to the fight club with Spike. Spike was a refreshing guy to be with—he didn't talk a lot, wasn't noticeably crazy, and didn't expect you to speak if there was nothing important to say.

Spike could also kick ass in the fight ring and go out for pizza. Broderick had joined him for the pizza tonight —anything to keep from heading home to his three pain-in-the-ass younger brothers, a half-feral Shifter Feline, and the half-feral's very protective human mate.

After he'd said good night to Spike, Broderick had dropped in on Sean Morrissey, the Shiftertown's Guardian, to report on ongoing tracker business. He'd sat with Sean on his back porch a while, watching Sean cuddle his sleeping cub on his lap.

Somewhere between saying good night to Sean and

heading home across the dark common yards behind Shifter houses, Broderick had lost consciousness.

The bands around his wrists were real—heavy-duty metal handcuffs. Strong enough for a Shifter, tight enough that even if he shifted to wolf, he wouldn't be able to slip his big paws out.

Broderick couldn't see and could barely breathe, because there was a bag over his head, its drawstring tight around his throat.

What the holy fuck?

Broderick's first instinct was to struggle, to break out of his restraints no matter how strong and kill whoever had done this. His second instinct told him to shut up and lie still and figure out where he was. No sense busting out of the cuffs and bag to find five guys with machine guns waiting for him. Cunning was sometimes the better part of valor.

Broderick remained motionless. He might not be able to see, but he could hear and he could scent, which for a Shifter, were more important senses at times like these.

He smelled humans, not in the room with him, but definitely nearby. His hackles rose. He doubted these humans were police or Shifter Bureau's mighty patrollers —*they'd* have put him into a sterilized cage, not bothering with the head bag. When he woke, a Shifter Bureau worker with a clipboard would explain why they'd decided to round him up, cage him, and terminate him.

So, if he hadn't been caught by Shifter Bureau or police, that left Shifter hunters.

Shifter hunters were humans who boasted of stalking un-Collared, rogue Shifters to bring them in or kill them. They weren't allowed to hunt Shifters with Collars, like Broderick, but because un-Collared Shifters weren't thick on the ground, the hunters often bent the rules. They'd go after anything Shifter, pretending not to notice that the Shifter they killed actually had a black and silver Collar around his neck. They'd apologize profusely, but said Shifter would already be dead.

Even as these thoughts formed, Broderick had his doubts. Hunters would have also stuck him into a cage or simply shot him. Besides, no way human hunters could have sneaked into Shiftertown. It was too well guarded by Shiftertown's trackers, of which Broderick was one.

Then who?

He felt cold stone under his body, smelled musty, dank air behind the head bag. Floorboards creaked, but overhead. He also smelled damp lint and laundry detergent, which meant a washing machine and dryer nearby. Conclusion—he was in somebody's basement.

Humans lived in this house, not Shifters. So again —*what the fuck?*

He smelled another odor, one of warm plastic, and he heard a hum of electronics. Interesting.

Broderick should have said *screw it* tonight and tried to see Joanne. He could be curled up on the sofa with her, watching TV, or ignoring the TV while they explored kissing and touching. Instead he'd been noble and left her alone. What was wrong with him?

A door scraped open, and footsteps headed down a flight of wooden stairs. Heavy treads, men, and the lighter tread of a female. The light steps moved swiftly past the heavy.

"Is this him?" the woman asked, breathless, eager.

Goddess, please don't tell me this is a Shifter groupie who wants a shag. I might throw up on her.

The bag loosened, and then was ripped from Broderick's head. He still couldn't see—a blindfold covered his eyes. Light penetrated the cloth, a very bright one, as though someone shone a flashlight on his face.

He felt breath touch his cheek, feminine, almost sweet, but cold and rapid with excitement. A small hand in his hair raised his head. Broderick suppressed his growl, his urge to snap out of the restraints and attack.

"Are you sure this is him?" the woman asked. She sounded young, especially for a human, past teen years, but not much. Broderick's head was moved left and right, the woman's breath coming faster. "Wait …" She released him abruptly, and Broderick's head clunked to the cement floor.

"What the hell did you bring me?" she demanded.

"The Shifter who came out of the Guardian's back door," a man answered. His voice was deep, holding strength, yet Broderick heard and smelled his fear. Of a woman not much older than a cub?

"This isn't him!" She climbed to her feet, her voice shrill. The flashlight beamed against Broderick's blindfold. "Does this *look* like a Feline? He's Lupine, you idiot."

"How the hell are we supposed to tell the difference?" the man asked with the annoyance of a scared person. "You didn't give us a picture to go by."

"Four Shifters live in that house," the young woman snapped. "Two are female. I would have thought you had at least a fifty-fifty chance of snatching the right *male*. But no, you had to bring me someone completely off the chart. He's obviously a grunt worker. No use to me at all!"

Was she insane? The two Shifters who lived in Sean's house were Sean, the Shiftertown Guardian, and his father, Dylan. If this woman's thugs had captured Dylan, he'd have killed her by now and all these guys too—and joined Spike for *three* pizzas. Sean wouldn't have been much safer for her, but maybe a little more polite before he left their bodies in broken piles.

Ah, the lucky sons of bitches. They'd snagged *Broderick* instead. He'd just bounce them around for fun and then call people to pick them up and charge them with hunting a Collared Shifter. Handy to know a guy in Shifter Bureau, one who wasn't a total dickhead.

"Get out!" the woman yelled at the men. "You useless shits; get the hell out!"

"You owe us." The tremor in the man's voice betrayed his fear, but he spoke with the determination of one who would do anything for money. "It wasn't easy to bring him here. Maybe he can help you anyway."

"Seriously?" the young woman cried. "I gave you half up front. The deal was the other half on delivery, but you didn't deliver, did you? If you come back with the right one, *maybe* I'll pay you. Or you can just get the hell out before I kill you."

Broderick heard a click of metal, the sound of a gun cocking.

"Whoa," the man said. "You are one crazy bitch. We're out of here."

He was walking even as he spoke. Footsteps sounded on the stairs, moving swiftly, then a door slammed. The floorboards creaked overhead, and then another above banged.

Broderick was left alone in the basement with an insane woman who had a gun. *Great.*

A slim hand hooked around the blindfold and tore it

away. Broderick blinked at the sudden glare of the flashlight, his mouth dry as linen.

When the light moved he could see the sharp-boned face of a young woman with short, unnaturally black hair. Her skin was fair and freckled, her mouth black with lipstick. The nails of the hand around the pistol had been painted black to match.

"No offense, Shifter," she said, her voice clear and youthful. She couldn't be more than twenty-something, the same age as Cherie, a young grizzly Shifter who lived not far from Broderick. "But I can't let you tell them about me."

Broderick could argue. He could say that a Shifter missing from Shiftertown would be a big deal, because they were all watched pretty closely. Joanne would worry when she couldn't reach Broderick, then she'd get his aunt worried, and then Aunt Cora would send his brothers to track him. When they started panicking, they'd go to Liam, who would organize a search. Tiger would get involved, and there was nowhere in the world this woman could hide from the messed-up shit that was Tiger.

But Broderick figured that argument would be a waste of breath. He wasn't good at arguing anyway.

He summoned all his Shifter strength, balled his fists, slammed his wrists apart, and rolled into the young woman's legs at the same time.

The cuffs remained whole, made to withstand Shifters, but Broderick's rolling bulk knocked the young woman off balance, and she went down.

Broderick kept moving. They hadn't bound his ankles, and he got his feet under him, one heavy boot kicking the gun out of the young woman's hand. The gun went off as her finger was tugged from the trigger, a bullet thudding into the wooden ceiling

She shouted vile words at him and scrambled to reach the gun. Broderick snarled in pain as he yanked at the cuffs again, calling on his strength to jerk free of them. He managed to break the chain between them, and now he had a matching pair of metal bracelets around his wrists.

Good enough. He'd done a quick assessment of the basement as soon as he could see and had already chosen his path of escape.

The long room had a washer and dryer standing on a cement platform on one end. Above these, at the top of the wall, were narrow windows leading outside. The rest of the room held tables upon tables of blinking computers, explaining the scent of warming plastic and the sound of working electronics.

Stacked CPU boxes flickered with lights, several monitors were pushed side-by-side, a few laptops were open, screens swirling with patterns, and keyboards lay here and there. The floor under the table was littered with junk—strands of wires, metal and plastic pieces, and small solid black boxes—a lot of stuff Broderick couldn't identify.

He took all this in between one heartbeat and the next, then he was across the room, on top of the washing machine, shifting to his between-beast, pulling the window out of its slot. He smashed glass and frame to the floor and the yard outside. The woman screamed.

She'd reached the gun. She fired two rounds as Broderick shifted completely to wolf and leapt for open air. His clothes finished shredding and falling away, and a sudden pain in his leg made him yelp.

The cuffs still clung to Broderick's wolf paws—the woman had judged the size and strength of them well. But he could squash himself flat if he needed to, and he did to scramble through the window, his most direct route of escape.

Pain burned in Broderick's leg as he scrambled out, but he made it. It was pitch dark, and Broderick had no idea where he was. Behind him, the woman was still screaming, still shooting, but the bullets pinged harmlessly inside the basement.

He stood up, panting. There were large houses nearby, but no lights shone in them, and they had the air of being empty, abandoned. Beyond them lay open fields of nothing. The young woman wasn't worried about anyone hearing her shooting, which meant these houses were a long way from anywhere.

Broderick didn't linger. He took off across the dirt and dried grass of the field on his swift wolf legs, scrambling over rocks and brush, putting as much distance between himself and the houses as he could.

Now to figure out where the hell he was and how he was going to get back to Shiftertown, alone, a wolf, with no clothes and no money.

And still this is better than being at home with that crazy-ass half-feral Shifter, Broderick thought as he limped on. *Damn, my life truly sucks.*

JOANNE GREENE ANSWERED THE PHONE WITH A sleepy, "Hello?" The bedroom of her north Austin house looked strange in the moonlight, sharp shadows on the wall like dancing ghosts.

"Joanne?" The worried tones of Broderick's Aunt Cora came across the line. "Is Broderick there with you?"

Joanne came alert at the note of fear in the woman's voice. Aunt Cora McNaughton was a small, take-no-shit woman with salt-and-pepper hair and clear gray eyes, who looked after Broderick and his brothers. When she sounded concerned, there was reason to be concerned.

"No," Joanne answered, her tone mirroring Cora's. "Or ..." Joanne slid out of bed, her cell phone pressed to her ear as she had a quick look around her small house. Broderick didn't always knock on the door and wait to be invited into a house like a normal person.

Joanne knew he wasn't there, though. Broderick had a presence, a power, that filled the house and was notably absent when he wasn't in it.

"He's not here," Joanne confirmed. "Why? What's wrong?"

"I don't know." Aunt Cora's voice trembled. "Maybe nothing. He vanished without saying a word to anyone and hasn't been seen since."

CHAPTER TWO

Broderick trotted across dry grasses in the dark for hours before he finally saw a smudge of light on the horizon. A town or city, its light glowing into the sky. What city, he had no idea, but once there, he'd at least be able to figure out where the hell he was. Humans liked to put large signs in front of their towns announcing the town's name, its population, and what it was famous for.

He'd decided that finding his way as wolf would be a better choice than trying to hitch a ride, stark naked. Drivers would take one look at him and call the police. Or they'd see the Collar and call Shifter Bureau.

Noses were better for finding the way out of a strange place anyway. Scent trails crisscrossed the land, invisible to human eyes, but to a wolf, they blazed like searchlights. Wolves were the best scent trackers ever made.

Broderick sat down on his haunches now to gaze across the rolling hills. At least he'd rid himself of the handcuffs. He'd shifted back to human and used the chain to pick open the cuffs' locks. He'd dropped the things to the bottom of a wash and gladly left them behind.

His paws were sore, something he'd never admit, but he'd be glad to curl up and sleep. It was wearying to be out here with no phone, no money, no way of knowing where he was, just his four feet and his nose to get him home.

Letting out a wolf sigh, he rose and moved down the slight rise he rested on and headed for the glow.

Disappointment hit him as he drew nearer. It wasn't a town at all, but some kind of power plant or chemical refinery, or whatever humans were doing in a place with smooth, cylindrical towers, lots of lights, and a fence around it.

He kept going. A plant meant a road and people with phones.

The fence around the place was formidable, he saw when he reached it—chain link interlaced with wires and topped with coils of barbed wire. Broderick could climb this, but he'd cut or fry himself doing it.

Better choice, he moved around to the entrance, keeping himself out of the glaring floodlights. Large gates, the kind that rolled back on tracks to admit trucks, blocked the way in. A guardhouse stood next to the entrance, square and impersonal, with a window and a door, and two armed guards lingering in front of it.

No sign graced the gates, which struck Broderick as odd. Humans liked to put signs on their factories as much as they did their towns. There was usually a name in fancy letters to tell everyone who they were and what they made.

The guards were alert but bored. Broderick read their apathy in their body language and in the scent that came to him on the wind. Nothing much was happening out here in the middle of the night.

Broderick flattened himself to the ground and approached the gatehouse at a low crawl. He stuck to shadows as much as he could, and came at it from an angle out of the guards' line of sight, or so he thought. Nowhere to hide out on the flat Texas plains.

"What was that?" One of the guards swung around, hand on gun, peering into the night.

"Just an animal," the other said. A flashlight flared. "See? Its eyes."

"What the hell kind of animal is that?"

Broderick stayed flat. Fear of wolves was entrenched in humans, after centuries of the animals eating their livestock, and many would shoot first, figure out what he was later.

"Coyote maybe?" the first guard continued.

Broderick bristled. Calling a Lupine a coyote was a grave insult. He made himself stay low however, pretending to be a wild whatever.

"Cool," the second guard said. Some humans had more curiosity about animals than fear. "Let me get a picture. My kids will love it."

Broderick sat up in the grass, giving him something at which to aim the camera in his phone. The first guard watched warily, but their pistols remained holstered.

Broderick wasn't after pistols, or blood, or human flesh. He was after what guard number two held in his hands.

Broderick charged. He could move faster than any human, and in a few seconds had knocked the flashlight out of the first guard's hand and had the second on the ground. Before either guard could recover, Broderick had the cell phone in his mouth and was sprinting back into the darkness.

"Hey!" A shot landed next to Broderick but missed him wildly. "Come back here! That stupid coyote ate my phone!"

Another shot, going even wider. Broderick was tired of people shooting at him tonight. The first guard was laughing, telling the second to holster it. Glad someone was having fun.

Broderick kept running. Behind him, the plant receded to a glow in the sky.

He eased off his pace and finally halted, dropping the phone out of his jaws so he could pant.

What the hell? The night had started off just fine. Out with his friends, besting others at the fight club, grabbing dinner with Spike and Spike's mate and their cute cub Jordan, hanging a little with Sean.

And then all this shit. Broderick heaved a sigh, and shifted to human. He grunted with the pain of the shift — some Shifters could do it smoothly, but Broderick was in the ranks of those who struggled.

The cell phone had GPS and a map, so Broderick could finally find out where he was. Looked like he was about a sixty miles or so from Austin, out in the hard plains of Texas west of San Antonio. Nearest paved road, twenty miles due east. Just perfect.

A giant *bang* had Broderick falling flat, instinct of several thousand years telling him to get down. The glow on the horizon flashed red, flames leaping high into the black and cloudless sky.

The plant had just blown up.

Broderick thought of the guards, both nervous and

bored, waiting for their shift to end. One wanted to take a picture of a coyote home to his kids.

"Aw, damn it." Broderick dropped the cell phone, painfully shoved himself into wolf form, tucked the phone back into his mouth, and ran for the plant.

He found the guards within a circle of flames, both of them on the ground, groaning. Black, fetid smoke rolled over them. Broderick got his teeth into the shirt of the one with kids and dragged him backward, out into the dried grasses and dirt beyond flames and smoke.

The other guard was struggling to breathe, his eyes closed, his face pasty. Broderick grabbed his shirt with his mouth, which pushed the phone further back behind his teeth. He'd probably swallow the damned thing and have a hell of stomachache.

Broderick dumped the first guard next to the second. Guard one did not look good. Guard two was awake, sitting up, coughing.

"Coyote?" the guard asked, voice rasping. "Shit, I'm sorry I shot at you."

Broderick dropped the phone out of his mouth, and strained back into human form. The guard reached for the dropped cell phone, not paying attention to Broderick in the dark, until Broderick snatched the phone from the man's outstretched fingers.

"*Wolf*," Broderick said in a hard voice. "Not *coyote*. Now be quiet, I need to make a call."

As the guard's jaw sagged, Broderick punched in Joanne's number, remembering it because he remembered everything about her. She answered right away.

"Who's this?"

She didn't sound half asleep, yanked from dreams,

pleasant or unpleasant. She was awake and already scared.

"It's Broderick, sweetie. Hey, I need you to come pick me up …"

"Out past the Fort Stockton turnoff? Near the munitions plant?"

"Munitions?" Broderick's gaze snapped to the fire. "That's not good. Wait a sec—how do you know where I am? *I* don't even know, not that specifically."

"Because every computer I own popped up an alert and I can hear emergency response on the scanners. At the same time, you call me on a phone in the plant's proximity. What the hell happened to you? Your aunt is here —she's worried sick."

Broderick heard the voice of his formidable aunt in the background. "Is he all right?" Aunt Cora was saying. "Where is he?"

Aunt Cora was about half the size of Broderick and his brothers, but she'd kept them in line for a hundred years and more. "Tell her I'm fine," Broderick said. "Any chance of a ride?"

"You didn't … you didn't have anything to do with the explosion, did you?" Joanne ventured.

"Hell, no. I wasn't anywhere near the place. I wouldn't be stupid enough to blow up a plant that makes *more* things that explode. Listen, baby, I'd love to talk, but I'd love more to get home and sleep. If you can't come out here, call Spike. He owes me—I paid for the pizza. Oh, and call Sean while you're at it. The crazy bitch who kidnapped me tonight was going for him, or his dad. Tell him to watch out."

"What? Broderick …?"

"Gotta go, baby. Cops are coming. I'll try to get to

that road, but my clothes are in shreds back wherever the hell I was. I'd borrow the uniforms of these guards here, but they won't fit. One of the guys seriously needs a hospital, so I'll be carrying him to an ambulance. See you, sweetie."

He heard Joanne yelling, spluttering as Broderick clicked off the phone.

"My girlfriend," Broderick said to the openmouthed guard. "She's going to kill me, but I'm too tired to care right now. We need to get him help."

Without waiting for the guard's response, Broderick handed him back the phone, hoping he'd ignore the teeth marks, and lifted the unconscious guard over his shoulder.

Broderick loped toward the approaching stream of fire trucks, police, and paramedics, waved down the paramedics, and laid the guard carefully on the ground next to the ambulance that pulled hurriedly to a halt. Broderick gave the emerging EMTs a wave, turned around, and ran back into darkness, shifting into wolf on the way.

JOANNE HUNCHED OVER THE STEERING WHEEL AS SHE went slowly down the highway, looking for signs of Broderick. She was alone—she'd sent Aunt Cora back to Shiftertown to convey Broderick's cryptic warning to Sean.

The crazy bitch who kidnapped me tonight was going for him.

What crazy bitch? *Kidnapped?* When the hell did Broderick get himself kidnapped? Joanne had been sleeping hard, her own life wearing her out, until Aunt Cora's phone call.

She saw him. Broderick rose from the grasses, in his wolf form, watching the headlights of her car approaching him.

Joanne knew this wasn't a wild wolf for several reasons—mainly, he was gigantic. Natural wolves were about two-thirds the size of a Shifter wolf. Second, the wolf didn't run away from the car, but calmly watched it approach. Most of all, when she pulled alongside him and stopped, the wolf morphed slowly into a very tall, very naked man.

"Hey, sweetie," he said, flashing her a Broderick grin. "Give me a lift?"

Joanne averted her eyes, though she couldn't help peeking. "There's clothes in the back."

Broderick looked good, as he always did, hard-bodied, not an ounce of fat on him. His muscles rippled as he walked, unashamed, around the car to the rear passenger door. He was limping, though, and Joanne saw blood on his leg.

Broderick opened the door and leaned in to get the jeans and shirt Joanne had brought. They were his— Broderick left a change of clothes at her place, in case he needed them after a shift, like now.

Broderick stretched the cotton T-shirt over his head and across his shoulders then unfolded it down his chest and abs. He ignored the underwear and pulled his jeans on over his bare butt, zipping and buttoning, then sliding in the belt she'd brought.

He stood looking around the open fields for a moment before climbing into the passenger seat. "All set. Thanks, baby. Can you take me back to Shiftertown?"

Joanne stared at him. Broderick settled himself comfortably on the seat, looking out the window, ready to go. Any moment now, he'd turn on the radio or start singing.

"Excuse me?" Joanne said. "What the hell?"

Broderick swung his head around to look at her. "*Excuse me,* what?"

"I'm waiting for you to tell me what happened! What crazy bitch kidnapped you? Why are you out here in the middle of nowhere—with a munitions plant blowing up? *Broderick!*"

He gave her a maddening stare. "I planned to talk while we were heading out of here. Before there are road-blocks or whatever because of the explosion."

"Which you had *nothing* to do with," Joanne said, uneasy.

"Nope. But do you expect cops to believe that from a Shifter? You can start any time now, sweetie."

"Why are you bleeding?" Joanne demanded.

"Hmm? Oh, that. A shot grazed me. It's already closed. Will you *go?*"

Joanne made an exasperated noise, put her car in gear, and headed down the narrow road, her headlights cutting a swath in the pitch dark.

"You were shot at?" she said. "By the police?"

"No, by the woman who kidnapped me. She didn't have all her oars in the water, I swear by the Goddess. Hey, you know about computers."

Joanne glanced at him. He was lounging comfortably, gazing down the highway as though they were going on a road trip, not heading swiftly away from a crime scene.

Joanne clenched the steering wheel. "Yes, I know about computers." She ought to. Joanne had trained as a programmer, became a very good one, and then got lured into the dark side by questionable friends in college. As a result, she'd learned how to be a very good hacker.

She'd hacked for the fun of it, until the day she realized it wasn't the "victimless" crime her associates had claimed it to be. A close non-programmer friend had lost everything—house, savings, insurance—her whole life— because of a huge hack attack that had taken her identity, drained her accounts, destroyed her credit, and left a trail of ruin in its wake. It had taken her two years to recover, with Joanne helping her every step of the way. Her friend now lived in New Mexico, where she'd had to start all over again.

From that time forward, Joanne was anti-hacker. She landed a job with a security testing firm that worked to help companies and individuals protect themselves and their information, and now she was a freelance consultant, working for herself. Joanne was good at it, though she knew that the very best thieves out there were hard to catch.

"So," Broderick was saying, "Why does someone need ten computers side by side in a basement? Compulsive online shopper?"

"No," Joanne said, her heart beating faster and her fingers tingling. "Sounds like they're setting up a network. Who was this woman?"

"Hell if I know. We didn't stop to exchange how-do-you-dos. She has black hair, black lipstick, tatts, but she's a baby, a cub. I bet not much past twenty."

"That's getting old for a hacker." Joanne pulled to a stop at a crossroads, looking out for traffic before she turned onto the bigger, four-lane highway. Nothing came at them but a lone car going the other direction. It soon passed, its passengers heading wherever at three o'clock in the morning.

"The question is, what does a hacker want with a Shifter?" Broderick asked.

"Maybe I can answer if you tell me what the hell happened to you!" Joanne said loudly, her patience gone.

Broderick held up his hands—there was bruising around his wrists. "Yeah, yeah, all right." He launched into a tale of innocently walking home from Sean's and waking up with his hands cuffed and a canvas bag on his head.

He spoke matter-of-factly, not playing up his heroics in breaking away, shrugging off the gunshot which had taken a piece of his flesh but did no more damage. He'd found his way to the plant, tricked the guards, grabbed their phone and ran off, then *ka-boom*.

Joanne listened, the tingle in her fingers increasing as it did when something both scared and excited her. She put together everything Broderick said, which to her led to one conclusion. "You said they meant to grab Sean and got you by mistake," she said. "Aunt Cora went to warn him."

"Good," Broderick said. "The men she hired were idiots though, if they couldn't tell a Lupine from a Feline."

"Not the point." Joanne found her foot going down on the pedal while her agitation rose. "She wanted *Sean*. Don't you get it? *He's* why a hacker needs a Shifter, Broderick. I bet she's going after every hacker's ultimate dream. She's planning to hack the Guardian Network."

CHAPTER THREE

B roderick stared at Joanne. He liked looking at her anyway, had since he'd met her.

When he'd first seen her, she'd been wearing groupie clothes, a tight dress that outlined every curve. Her hair had been as black as that of the woman who'd kidnapped him tonight, but in the nearly ten months he'd known Joanne, she'd let the dark brown that was her true color take over, though she kept her hair short. She had large brown eyes, which she'd changed to blue with contacts when she'd been in disguise as a groupie, but she'd since discarded.

Broderick liked her natural look better. Now she was all *her*. On the other hand, he wouldn't mind if she wore the skimpy pink groupie dress now and again. But, she looked just as good to him in a sloppy T-shirt and denim shorts.

All this flashed through Broderick's thoughts while Joanne's words penetrated his brain. He started shaking his head. "No way. No one can hack the Guardian

Network. It's got Fae magic shit built into it. That's what I hear, anyway."

Joanne's look was thoughtful. "I bet it can be hacked if you have a Guardian tied up and threatened."

"It would take a lot to threaten Sean. He'd eat the woman for breakfast."

"Well, it sounds to me like she wants to have a good try at breaking into the network. What if she threatens Sean's mate to get him to cooperate? Or his son?"

"Yeah." Broderick's uneasiness grew. "I say we get back to Shiftertown as fast as we can and see what's up."

"On it," Joanne said, and the car sped up.

———

JOANNE DIDN'T WANT TO GO *TOO* FAST, BECAUSE BEING pulled over for speeding, plus having to explain why she was driving around with a Shifter in the middle of the night was not what she needed.

There was no mistaking Broderick for anything but a Shifter. He had the look—gray eyes that bore a wildness that had never been tamed, dark hair buzzed short, a hard face, and a big, tough body. The clincher was the Collar that rested around Broderick's neck, a Celtic knot at his throat.

The Collars contained technology and Fae magic that sent shocks through any Shifter who started to grow too violent. Shifters, however, had found ways around the Collar problem. Joanne had seen Broderick battle hard at the fight club without the shocks slowing him down too much. Afterward, he would hurt—Collar hangover, he called it. During the fight, though, he didn't let his Collar slow him down.

Driving as fast as Joanne dared on the wandering back highways put them in the outskirts of Austin in an hour. At this time of night, traffic was fairly light, and she soon crossed town and turned onto the side streets that led to Shiftertown.

The bar on the corner just outside Shiftertown was dark, closed, everyone gone home. Shiftertown itself was quiet except for flashes of big cats roaming the yards of the tidy bungalows.

Broderick's house was large, two-story, with space needed for Broderick, his three younger brothers, his aunt, and now Joanne's sister and her mate, whom Broderick had rescued a few months ago.

Broderick had volunteered to let Aleck stay with him —there was not much room in any other Shifters' houses, and Aleck needed to be under Shifters' watchful eye while they tried to cure him. Plus, Joanne knew Broderick had done it for her, because of Nancy. She would ever be grateful to him for that.

Broderick was out of the car as soon as it stopped. A human man might have come around to Joanne's side and opened the door for her, or at least waited until she was out, before approaching the house, but Shifter rules of etiquette were different. Shifter males always forged ahead to scout, to make sure the way was safe for their females and cubs. Didn't matter that this was Broderick's own house with his aunt and brothers inside—instinct told him to look anyway. And who knew? Rival Shifters could have taken over his home and be waiting to ambush him.

Once Broderick had the front door open and had checked inside, he came back out and waved Joanne up to the porch.

Joanne slammed her car door and hurried to him. Before Broderick could walk into the house, Joanne flung her arms around his neck, dragging him close. "Damn it, Broderick, I was so worried about you!"

She felt him start, then still. Joanne hugged him tighter. After a moment, Broderick's arms came around her, hesitant, then stronger.

"I'm okay, sweetheart," he said, sounding puzzled. "It was just a nick. She missed."

Joanne lifted her head and thumped her fists softly on his chest. "No, you idiot. I mean, you were abducted and taken prisoner. I might never have seen you again."

Broderick had a stunned look on his face, as though surprised she cared. Very surprised. "I'm all right. I got away easy."

Joanne pushed from him. "You are so …" She made an exasperated noise. "And what you call *easy* scares the shit out of me." She shoved past him and into the house, feeling his stare on her back all the way.

Joanne didn't really blame Broderick for being surprised at her reaction. They didn't have that kind of relationship, not one in which Joanne kissed him hello when he came over and asked how his day was then fixed him a hot meal before they went to bed for all-night passion. Nor was it one where Broderick brought her flowers and expensive jewelry and took her to fancy restaurants — before returning home for all-night passion.

Going out with a Shifter was a little more compli-cated. Shifters weren't allowed into most fancy restau-rants, and they didn't understand that flowers and jewelry were gifts a woman would want. A Shifter's idea of showing affection was keeping the woman safe from enemies. Gifts — presenting her with an object treasured

in their family for centuries. That was Shifter-style
dating. The gift giving usually only happened after
mating, though, when the male Shifter's mate of choice
had joined the family. The whole family. Shifters living
alone with their mates was a weird idea to them.

Nancy, Joanne's older sister, loved everything about
Shifters. Joanne was learning, little by little, how to
appreciate them.

Broderick strode in behind Joanne, his voice gruff.
"Aunt Cora, did you talk to Sean?"

"Of course I did." Aunt Cora, who was smaller than
her nephews but who'd managed to keep them in line
before and after their mother had passed, came out of the
kitchen. She had coffee, which Joanne fell upon grate-
fully. "Why wouldn't I?" Aunt Cora asked. "Sean thanked
me, but didn't sound unduly worried."

"Felines." Broderick grabbed a cup and drank noisily.
"Human men with weapons managed to grab me in the
middle of Shiftertown, and *he's* not worried. Joanne
thinks they're after more than just messing with Shifters."

"All right, then *you* talk to Sean," Aunt Cora said.
"Now that you're home safe, I'm going to bed."

Broderick went to his aunt and caught the small
woman in a tight, smothering hug, holding his coffee out
of the way. He had no shame in showing affection for
Aunt Cora. From what Joanne understood, after Broderick's father had been killed years ago, his mother had lost
a lot of strength, and Aunt Cora, his father's sister, had
taken care of them all. Broderick's mother had passed in
the last year. When the mate bond was severed, Joanne
had seen, the remaining Shifter could succumb to
hard grief.

Broderick released his aunt and swung away, lifting

his coffee to his lips. Aunt Cora gave his back an affectionate look.

"Is Nancy up?" Joanne asked her.

Aunt Cora nodded, her expression turning sympathetic. "Probably. Aleck's having a bad night, and Nancy's worried about you."

Joanne thanked her. It was typical of Nancy to sit up with her mate, who might die and sever *her* mate bond, but yet spare plenty of worry for her little sister.

Joanne set her coffee cup down, said good night to Broderick as he headed for the porch, and went up the stairs. She felt Broderick turn to watch her, but he said nothing other than to rumble *good night*, didn't follow her or try to stop her.

Typical of him. Broderick could be affectionate, but much of the time, he acted as though he didn't know what to do with Joanne. It was maddening, but then again, Broderick had brought Joanne's sister and mate, Aleck, home without fuss, making sure they were looked after.

Well, maybe not *without fuss*, but Broderick could have foisted them off on any of the other Shifters, and he hadn't. He had no obligation to look after Joanne's family, and yet, he never insisted they leave.

Joanne knew which bedroom upstairs had been redone for her sister and Aleck, who battled with going feral.

When a Shifter went feral, he or she reverted to the wild creature inside and forgot how to be human. Shifters had originally been bred by the Fae as Battle Beasts, animals who could fight with the swiftness and strength of large predators but have the sentience and cunning of humans.

Shifters had come a long way since then, fighting free

of their Fae masters and setting up home in the human world. They'd lived more or less like humans for centuries —moving into human homes, embracing their fashions, food, entertainment, and culture.

At the same time, Shifters would never be completely human. The animals inside were their true selves. When a Shifter went feral, he reverted to the Battle Beast, living on instinct alone, becoming a danger to everyone around him, even his own family.

Aleck was a special case, even for a feral. Aleck didn't have a Collar, hadn't worn one in his life. He'd evaded the humans who rounded up all Shifters into Shiftertowns and had lived with a group of Shifters in his same situation. Led by a white tiger called Kendrick, who was also a Guardian, they'd found places to hide, moving whenever their strongholds were in danger of being discovered. Joanne had helped on the raid that had found the un-Collared Shifters and Nancy, who had stayed with them to be with Aleck.

Nancy came out of the bedroom before Joanne reached it, her abdomen protruding with the cub she carried, Aleck's. She was due soon.

Nancy enclosed Joanne in an embrace, warm and scented with the honey shampoo she liked. "You okay, Jo-Jo?"

As always, Joanne was torn between relief, love, and anger when she was with Nancy. The fact that Nancy hadn't confided in her about Aleck, leaving Joanne hanging and believing Nancy had been abducted, still rattled her, even though Nancy's reasons for keeping quiet had been sound. On the other hand, having Nancy safe and back in her life again made Joanne rejoice. Sister stuff was complicated.

"I'm fine," Joanne said as they ended the hug. "Broderick ... He's fine too. How's Aleck?"

Nancy's eyes softened at the mention of her mate's name, then she looked worried. "He didn't know where he was for a while tonight. He's better now, but I can't be away from him long."

Joanne squeezed her sister's hands. "I'm sorry, Nance. I wish there was something I could do."

"He's held on this long." Nancy sounded confident, though her eyes were moist. "Sean says he and Andrea might be close to a breakthrough."

Joanne would believe that when she saw it. Andrea was Sean's mate, a half-Fae, half-Shifter woman who had healing powers, but so far those powers had not been enough to jolt Aleck back to sanity. She knew, though, that the Shifters were trying.

"Want me to stay with you tonight?" Joanne asked. "I'm already here."

Nancy shook her head. "You have your own life, Jo-Jo."

So Nancy claimed. But Joanne's parents had charged Joanne to look after Nancy when the sisters had moved to Austin to attend UT, find jobs, and begin their lives. While Nancy was two years older than Joanne, she'd been the wild one, younger Joanne more responsible and stable. Even in her hacker years, Joanne had been careful, reliable, and had held a good-paying job while Nancy toured the world with her musician boyfriend and then became a Shifter groupie after that breakup.

"Not much of a life," Joanne said. "I'm happy to look out for you, Nance."

Nancy rubbed Joanne's shoulders. "Don't say that. Broderick likes you, and you're welcome here. No matter what, Shifters will always open their homes to you. You've proved you're their friend."

Nancy lived with stars in her eyes. "Not really," Joanne said. "When you were missing, I was a real pain in the ass to the Shifters here. I put them in danger. Not understanding the danger I was sending to them is no excuse. They put up with me coming here because of you."

Nancy gave her a wise look. "I think you're wrong about that, but I know you won't listen. If you stay here tonight, you can use the extra bed in Aunt Cora's room. She won't mind."

Nancy had this idea that Shifters were one, big, happy family and would open their homes and their hearts to Nancy's family too. It must be nice to be so certain of life.

"I'll ask her," Joanne said, more cautious. While Aunt Cora had made it clear she liked Joanne and Nancy, Broderick's younger brothers were not as thrilled with having humans in their house, not to mention a half-feral Feline. And who knew what Broderick himself would think of her staying?

Nancy hugged Joanne again. "Good night, then. Have to get back to Aleck."

Joanne said good night after the hug and watched her sister slip back into the bedroom at the end of the hall. In spite of moving awkwardly with her advanced pregnancy and having a mate who was slowly going insane, Nancy looked happy. Happier than she'd ever been. If Joanne could experience even half that contentment, her life would be good.

BRODERICK STRODE OUT ONTO THE FRONT PORCH after Aunt Cora and Joanne went upstairs. He'd finished off his coffee, which made him restless, as did the aftermath of his escape, his run through the wilderness, the incidents at the plant, and finally making it back home. His lower calf had a new gash, but he'd be fine.

He should crash now, sleeping off the night and the pain his Collar had dug into him when he'd fought his way out of the house.

Instead, he kept feeling Joanne's arms around him, hearing the throb in her voice when she said *Damn it, Broderick, I was so worried about you!*

No one worried about Broderick. Aunt Cora, maybe, but in a different way. No one cared much about the hard-ass Lupine who fought tough, talked loud, and went home alone every night.

His mouth said things before his brain could get him to shut up. He'd always thought the only way to find a mate was to mate-claim a woman and then meet any Challenge for her. How else was he going to get a female to actually move in with him?

And then, he'd met Joanne. From the beginning, he'd been drawn to her. Maybe because all of Shiftertown was angry at her, and Broderick, knowing what that felt like, had decided to stand up for her.

She'd acted against the Shifters from fear, not malice. Once Joanne had understood that *they* hadn't abducted her sister, she'd done all she could to make it right. Shifters were still pissed off at her, but they understood they'd have to go through Broderick to achieve any retaliation. And he wasn't going to let them.

Broderick saw movement in the darkness. He came alert, pain forgotten, but he recognized Spike at the end of the walk. Another Shifter hulked beside him, and Broderick groaned inwardly.

Spike and Tiger waited for Broderick to allow them onto his territory. Broderick was known for being unforgiving to those who crossed the line without his permission.

He waved them up to the porch, too tired to play belligerent alpha tonight. Spike approached with his usual saunter, which belied his powerful swiftness. Tiger never hid anything. He was big, strong, and could break every one of Broderick's bones if he chose.

Both Shifters climbed to the porch. Spike leaned against the railing, crossing his motorcycle-booted feet. Starlight gleamed on Spike's shaved head, the tattoos that covered his arms blending into the darkness. Spike's entire body was tattooed, with the exception of his hands and feet.

Tiger simply stood there like a monolith. His unruly hair was black streaked with orange-red. He was bigger than most Shifters except the bears—he was about the same size as Ronan. Tiger was the strongest Shifter Broderick knew, and many Shifters were still wary about him. His mate, on the other hand, loved him to pieces. Tiger wasn't an aggressive alpha, in spite of his size and strength, wasn't hostile, threatening. Tiger wasn't anything. He was … Tiger.

"Just came from Sean," Spike said after they'd been quiet a moment. "He's not happy."

"Didn't think he would be." Broderick rested his hands on the porch railing. It needed paint—he'd have to take time to do that, or else order his brothers to sand and refinish it. "Joanne thinks this woman with the computers is trying to hack the Guardian Network."

Spike's brows went up at that. "Huh. That could be very, very bad." He hesitated. "Dylan wants to know how the hell you let someone sneak up on you and bag you."

"Fuck if I know." Broderick hated the fact that someone had. "They didn't follow us to Shiftertown. We'd have known. I bet they snuck in here while all of us were at the fight club, then waited. Ask Dylan how the hell did he let humans hang out here to ambush me? They tran-qued me—must have. They were fast."

"I'm not asking Dylan that, not in those words," Spike said. "But it's a good question."

Broderick grunted "Dylan's distracted. What with chasing around un-Collared Shifters and having a mate that drives him nuts, I can't blame him for slipping."

Spike chuckled, which was unbending for him. "I'm not saying that to him either. He says we need to find this woman and her lair. Could you get back there if you had to?"

Broderick considered. "Maybe. Take me a while to backtrack. I don't want to go near that munitions plant anytime soon. If the cops think a Shifter was nearby, we're all in deep shit." Police would swarm into Shifter-town and question everyone, from Dylan all the way down to the newest born cub.

"Helping you backtrack is where Tiger comes in," Spike said. "He can track anything."

Tiger fixed Broderick with a stare. "I need a scent."

Broderick shrugged. "All the clothes I was wearing are in tatters in her basement. She has my wallet and phone too. The woman knows everything about me. Which makes me uncomfortable." *The understatement of the day.*

"Don't need your clothes," Tiger said. "Just the scent."

Broderick's head came up. "Aw, no way am I letting the crazy *sniff* me."

"Suck it up," Spike said. "You fight him in the ring. What's the difference?"

"Big difference, and you know it."

Spike was enjoying himself. Broderick hadn't seen him this chuffed since he'd brought home his cub and got himself a mate.

Tiger didn't wait for permission. He stepped to Broderick, put his giant hand on the back of Broderick's neck, and pulled him close.

CHAPTER FOUR

Broderick felt Tiger's scalding breath on his neck then his shoulder. Broderick very carefully stood motionless, not jerking away.

If any other Shifter had dragged Broderick close and inhaled his scent, said Shifter would be on the ground. But Tiger wasn't like other Shifters. He'd been made in a lab, created by a mishmash of genetic material and the Goddess knew what else. He'd been part of an experiment to manufacture a Shifter army, which hadn't worked at all. The first twenty-two experiments had died, leaving Tiger alone. The poor guy didn't even have a real name, and no family or clan. Broderick couldn't imagine the loneliness. As much as Broderick's brothers drove him spare, he wouldn't trade any of them for what Tiger had gone through.

Tiger finished with Broderick's neck, then he stooped and took the scent of Broderick's throat. Finally, he stood up and stepped away, in no way awkward.

Spike watched, his arms folded, an amused look on

his face. "Wish I had a camera," he said. "Did you get enough, Tiger?"

Tiger nodded, offering no apology.

Spike went on. "Dylan wants this woman brought in. As soon as possible, he said. With Dylan, that means *right now.*"

Broderick rubbed the back of his neck, where the sensation of Tiger's ultra-strong hand lingered. "She won't be at that house anymore. She'll have run by now."

Tiger shrugged. "Then we'll follow her."

"Tomorrow," Broderick said firmly, although that was only a few hours away. "I want her too, but I've been shot, need to recover, and I'm half dead on my feet."

"And your mate is here," Tiger said, perfectly serious.

Broderick growled. "She's not my —"

"Yes, she is." Tiger gave Broderick his unnerving yellow stare.

"That's not how it works." Broderick didn't know why he got squirrelly every time someone mentioned *mates* and Joanne, but he did. Probably because he was pretty sure she'd refuse him. "You mate-claim a female, then if no one Challenges, you have the sun and moon ceremony, and *that* makes her your mate."

Tiger listened as though Broderick offered profound wisdom, then he gave a slight shake of his head. "She's your mate."

Broderick abruptly changed the subject. "Does Sean know to keep his ass hidden?" he asked Spike. "In case the kidnappers try again?"

Spike shrugged, his tight shoulders moving. "Sean's not sure what to believe. That's why Dylan wants the girl brought in."

"Sure. We'll abduct a human, tie her up, drag her to

Shiftertown, and question her. I don't mind, because she pissed me off, but why can't Dylan do his own dirty work?"

"Because he's Dylan, and we're the lowly trackers." Spike pried himself from the railing. "Get some sleep—we'll go right after breakfast. Most humans are at their jobs by then and maybe we won't get stuck in as much traffic."

"So, what if the Guardian Network did get hacked?" Broderick asked curiously. "Is it that big a deal? It's just a database of information about Shifters, right? Shifter Bureau already has all our deets on file. What else could she find out?"

"Hell if I know," Spike said. "It's a big Guardian secret what's really in that database. Maybe there's nothing to steal. She might be chasing rainbows."

"Or sees them floating around her head," Broderick said. "She was stark-raving bonkers, but aren't most humans?"

Spike only made a noncommittal gesture. He was mated to a human, and she'd bring in his second cub sometime this summer. Tiger didn't answer, but he didn't always talk.

Broderick and Spike agreed on the time to meet in the morning, and Spike and Tiger made to depart. At the bottom of the porch steps, Tiger turned back.

"The Guardian Network holds the secrets," he said. Then he walked away, passing Spike in the darkness, and was gone.

Spike flashed a *no idea what he's on about* look over his shoulder, and jogged across the street in Tiger's wake.

Broderick remained on the porch, enjoying the cool air for a while, wondering what the hell Tiger meant.

Tiger loved to spring these cryptic pieces of information on Broderick, to make Broderick's head hurt trying to figure them out. Tiger always proved to be right no matter how obscure the problem, and Broderick had learned not to argue with him.

But if he conceded Tiger might be right about the Guardian Network, then he'd have to agree that Tiger's conviction that Joanne was Broderick's mate was true as well.

No question. *Damn the furry, tiger-striped bastard.*

———

"HELL, YES, I'M GOING WITH YOU," JOANNE TOLD Broderick over her first cup of coffee. Aunt Cora had been up with the sun, in spite of the late night, handing Joanne a welcome, steaming mug as she stumbled into the kitchen after showering and dressing.

Broderick, the big lump, was polishing off a heaping plate of bacon and eggs, telling Aunt Cora that he and Spike and Tiger were going after his kidnappers this morning. When Joanne said she wanted to accompany him — she could look at the woman's computers and figure out what she was up to — Broderick came on all alpha male.

"No," he said in a stern voice. "Too dangerous."

Joanne thumped down across from him. The sunny kitchen sported a long, old wooden farm table, scrubbed and scraped over the years. Aunt Cora kept it strewn with straw placemats, and she'd tied bright red-gingham cushions to the seats of the heavy wooden chairs. The kitchen was always warm and gleaming, copper pots hanging over the stove, the smell of something good baking in the oven. Joanne had spent her youngest years in her grandmother's farmhouse kitchen in north Texas, and Aunt Cora's always filled her with nostalgia.

This morning, however, Broderick was pushing nostalgia away and filling Joanne with irritation.

"Do you know another computer hacker as good as me who can help you?" Joanne demanded.

"Yes." Broderick took a calm mouthful and swallowed. "The woman Pablo Marquez lives with. Forget her name. She's supposed to be very good."

Pablo was a crime lord, a leader of some very bad men, who, it was true, kept others even worse in line. Pablo had helped Shifters a time or two, but always reluctantly. From what little Joanne had seen of him, he was very protective of his family, matching even the protectiveness of Shifters.

"Right." Joanne scowled at Broderick. "Pablo is going to loan out his girlfriend to help you go after a dangerous hacker, because he's so in love with Shifters."

Broderick hesitated. "Well, I haven't exactly asked him yet. We wanted to grab the woman first."

"Why wait?" Joanne plunked her coffee mug to the straw mat. "I'm the best person besides Sean you have on hand for anything computer-related. And it's not like I'm bad at going into danger. I helped you find my sister, didn't I?"

As Broderick's brows drew together, Joanne thought maybe that hadn't been the best argument. Joanne had let herself be taken by the un-Collared Shifters back to their bunker, with a tracker in her pocket, where they'd found Nancy. The tracker hadn't been Broderick's idea — that had been Walker's instinct during the situation. Walker was a Special Forces guy, who'd been assigned to the hunt for Nancy and had come with all sorts of toys that helped them breach the compound.

Broderick had been very upset at Walker for leaving Joanne with the Shifters. "Yeah," he said now. "And I'm still not happy about that."

In spite of his bad temper and having been abducted and shot, Broderick looked none the worse for wear this morning. In fact he looked good, a treat for the eyes. His short dark hair was damp from a shower, and he'd shaved, which emphasized the strong bones of his face. His body was just as strong, biceps stretching the short sleeves of his T-shirt. He had tatts on his arms, flames and one of a dragon that looped its tail around his wrist. Shifters liked tattoos, which, for some reason, did not remain when they became their animals.

Broderick's gray eyes were free from the pain Joanne had seen in him last night, though the rage about his abduction remained. He extended that anger to Joanne now, his protective instincts rising.

Aunt Cora shoveled a large mountain of scrambled eggs onto a plate for Joanne. Shifters didn't believe in skimpy portions. "Take her with you," she said to Broderick. "I'll worry about you less if Joanne goes along. I can at least trust her to keep you alive and out of trouble."

Broderick gave his aunt a weary glance as she approached the table. "Aunt Cora …"

Aunt Cora firmed her mouth. "Either she goes, or you tell Dylan to fetch this girl himself."

Broderick had a stare-down with her, which he lost. On purpose, Joanne knew. Broderick was the alpha of the group without question, but Aunt Cora was special to him. He snarled under his breath and returned his focus to his breakfast. "I can't believe the shit I put up with …"

"You'll put up with a lot more if you don't take Joanne," Aunt Cora growled. She shoved Joanne's breakfast in front of her and went back to making more for Broderick's brothers, who hadn't appeared yet. "If Joanne doesn't go, *I* will."

Broderick sent her an alarmed look. "You can't," he said flatly.

"Try and stop me."

Broderick heaved a long, heavy, aggrieved sigh. "All right, all right. Joanne can come." He pointed a thick finger across the table at her. "But you stay back and stay safe. No running off on your own trying to find the woman or catch her. You got that?"

"Am I supposed to say, *Yes, sir?*" Joanne lifted her fork and batted her eyelashes. "Or, *Yes, dear?*"

"Yeah, yeah, you're funny."

Joanne flashed him a triumphant look and attacked her meal. She'd never eat it all, but she knew that Broderick or the three brothers who pushed their way into the kitchen would.

Broderick's brothers were still uncertain about Joanne, and she wasn't entirely comfortable with them yet. The McNaughtons were a close family, but they were rough-and-tumble close, which Joanne wasn't used to. Her own upbringing had been sedate. She and Nancy, though very different, had never had a problem showing their love for each other. Broderick and his brothers took a different approach, usually a loud one.

The youngest was Mason. He was just past his Transition and ready to take on the world. He walked in a restless slouch to plop down in a chair next to Joanne, giving her his unnerving gray stare.

The next brother up was Derek, who was around

fifty, which was still young for a Shifter—Broderick was a hundred something. He was the wildest of the brothers, Joanne had come to learn, disappearing for days at a time. No one worried about him—even Aunt Cora knew he'd turn up, hungry and exhausted and sleep for a day and a half. Broderick gave him grief, saying he could get the family, maybe all Shifters in deep shit if he wasn't careful, and Derek would growl at him to mind his own business.

Next up was Corey, nearly a hundred. He never said much. He resembled Broderick the most, but he had a completely different personality. Where Broderick blustered, Corey was quietly competent. He won plenty of fights at the fight club without much fuss. He'd never go up against Broderick, though.

None of the brothers fought each other at the fight club, and Broderick wouldn't let Mason even enter the rings. While it was a rule of the club that winning a fight did not change the dominance level of a Shifter, there was always the underlying awareness that it did. Broderick's family was uneasy enough as it was—challenging each other's dominance at the fight club would stir up trouble at home, and all of them knew it.

Privately, Joanne thought that the brothers simply knew that Broderick would always be able to kick their asses. They didn't want their faces rubbed in that truth, so they obeyed him without fuss.

"Hey, Joanne." Derek paused to rub her shoulder.

Joanne knew enough about Shifters by now to understand that Derek wasn't coming on to her. Shifters communicated a lot by touch, used it to soothe, and as a sign of acceptance. Derek was showing he approved of her being here.

Broderick glanced at him, but said nothing. Derek continued his massage, which Joanne admitted felt good. Mason and Corey said nothing to Joanne at all, though they both gave her perfunctory nods.

Joanne was right that the brothers finished her half-eaten plate of food. After breakfast was done, she ran upstairs to hurry through teeth brushing and saying good-bye to Nancy, who briefly emerged from Aleck's room to see her. Joanne raced downstairs again, certain Broderick would leave without her if she dawdled.

Broderick waited for her on the porch. A little surprised he'd not ditched her, Joanne smiled at him. "Let's go kick some hacker ass," she said.

Broderick didn't return the smile. "You leave ass kicking to me and the Shifters. Any sign of trouble, you get down and stay down."

"I'm not completely stupid," Joanne said, her frown coming on. "Then again, *I'm* not the one who got shot last night."

She'd meant only to tease him, but Broderick's face turned an interesting shade of red. He came at her, wrapped strong hands about her waist, lifted her, and sat her butt on the railing of the porch.

"This isn't a game, Jo-Jo. You could get *hurt*. If you think it didn't kill me when Walker left you alone in that Shifter bar—and I knew I might never see you again—you'd be wrong."

The growl in Broderick's voice was fierce, his eyes changing from dark gray to light like mist as he pushed his face close to hers.

"But I was all right," Joanne said, gentling her voice. "Walker knew I would be, or he wouldn't have left me."

"I don't agree. Walker would have done any damn

thing to fulfill his mission and to impress that Kodiak she-bear he pants after."

"And I knew you'd come for me," Joanne said.

Broderick stilled, his eyes changing back to the smoky color she liked. "You're damn right I did."

Broderick kissed her—a hard, raw kiss that scraped her lips and made them ache. Joanne's head went back under the onslaught, caught by his strong hand.

As quickly as it started, the kiss ended. Broderick released her, breathing hard, as he ran his fingertips down Joanne's cheek, the caress firm.

"Spike's here," he said abruptly. Broderick brushed another kiss over her burning lips then turned and walked down off the porch.

Joanne gulped air, her heart pounding as she grabbed the railing to steady herself. She watched Broderick striding toward the edge of the yard, raising a broad hand in greeting to Spike, Tiger, and another Shifter, Seamus. Like Aleck, Seamus didn't wear a Collar, never had one. The fake he'd been given gleamed on his neck.

"Don't mind Brod." Mason's voice sounded abruptly behind her, making Joanne give a little yip of surprise. Mason stood behind the front screen door, its mesh softening his bulk. "He never knows which way his head is screwed on."

Joanne fumbled for words. "I … Yeah. He's fine."

"He goes hot and cold, because he's pretty sure you'll dump him in the end," Mason went on. "He's really bad at relationships."

"Mason." Aunt Cora joined him behind screen. "When you try looking for a mate, boyo, you'll understand how tough it is. Better go on, Joanne. And take care of him."

Aunt Cora laid her hand on Mason's shoulder, more

or less dragged him back into the house, and shut the front door.

Joanne let out a breath, taking in Mason's declaration, then she turned and ran on sneakered feet to meet Broderick.

Broderick was looking over the collected Shifters and the battered black truck they were apparently to use.

"Great," he said. "I'm going out hunting with an empath, a fight club champion, a crazy tiger, and my girlfriend. We can't lose."

CHAPTER FIVE

Tiger was a frigging genius with automobile engines, so the truck, while outwardly ratty, ran with a purr. Spike drove, and Tiger and Seamus sat in the bed. The cab was technically too small for Spike, Joanne, and Broderick together, but Broderick squeezed in, not wanting Joanne riding in the cab without him.

Not that Spike was a threat—the man was happy with his mate, Myka, his cub, Jordan, and a cub on the way. Broderick simply didn't want to take his eyes off Joanne. The last time she'd accompanied him on a mission, Broderick had nearly lost her. He damn well wasn't going to let that happen again.

Broderick recalled the smash-and-grab raid Walker had led on the bunker containing the un-Collared Shifters and Broderick's gut-punching relief when he'd found Joanne curled up in a chair in the bunker, unhurt. Broderick had wanted to put her over his shoulder and haul her out of there immediately, but Joanne had dragged them to her sister, whom she'd found tending Aleck.

Broderick had got all three of them out of there,

miraculously. Okay, so maybe Walker and Rebecca had helped a little, but the point was, they'd made it out.

Broderick slid closer to Joanne where she sat between him and Spike. Joanne glanced at him, and Broderick warmed when she put her hand on his thigh.

Spike, unaware of or uncaring of Broderick's messed up thoughts, drove them, at Joanne's direction, to the highway where she'd picked up Broderick. This morning, the road lay quietly under a wide sky, the occasional car or truck rumbling past where they'd pulled over. Wildflowers dotted the side of the road, bluebonnets brushing the grasses.

Broderick emerged from the truck, Joanne right behind him. Broderick stretched his back from the cramped ride. "That direction," he said, pointing over empty land, tinged green and blue. "I came across the fields from the munitions plant. Anyone hear why that blew up?"

Seamus had slid out of the truck and now lounged against it. "Bree was listening to the news this morning. She says they don't know what happened, but suspect a fire in one of the labs. There were some injuries, but no one was killed, fortunately."

Which meant that the guard Broderick had dragged toward the ambulance hadn't died either. He paused a moment to express thanks to the Goddess. Those men, just doing their jobs, hadn't deserved such a fate.

"Can you be more specific?" Spike asked Broderick, his gaze on the empty fields. "That's a hell of a lot of space to explore."

"That way." Tiger had climbed out behind Seamus, and now he pointed with a blunt finger to the southwest.

"Yeah?" Spike asked in irritation. "How do I go *that way*?"

Tiger shrugged, the big man rippling muscle. "There must be roads."

"Oh, for heaven's sake." Joanne had her phone out, manipulating the screen with her fingers. Broderick looked over her shoulder at the map she brought up.

"This is where we are," she said, pointing to two white streaks of roads that crossed. "The munitions plant is there." She swiped the screen to show a lone building. "Go around that way to get to it." Joanne indicated a grid.

Spike glanced at the map, as mystified as Broderick. "You navigate," Spike said to Joanne. "Just tell me where to turn."

They piled back into the truck, Joanne keeping an eye on her phone. Following her directions, Spike reached the munitions plant, which involved miles on a series of dirt roads.

Spike stopped when the plant was in sight, but far enough away that they'd not be spotted by guards. The place was still surrounded by emergency vehicles and too many cops for Broderick's taste. The police would have to investigate, of course. A factory that made bullets and explosives blowing up might mean bad luck or it might mean an outside enemy was trying to destroy it.

Spike drummed his fingers on the wheel. "All right, so how'd you end up *here*?"

Broderick got out and looked around. He'd been heading east, the setting moon at his back, when he made it to the plant, but *east* covered a lot of area. He didn't pick up any scent of himself, so he hadn't come out at this spot. The others waited, saying nothing, but Broderick sensed their growing impatience.

What did they expect him to do—shift to wolf and sniff himself out in these miles of nothing? The swath of dried grasses, touched with green, spread to the horizon. The sky was endless today, a soft blue that dwarfed the Shifters, the factory, the land, and the battered pickup.

"Kind of *that way*," Broderick said, fluttering his fingers.

Tiger walked around the truck, and around it again in a widening circle. He scanned the ground, land, horizon, his golden eyes taking in everything.

Tiger finally stopped and pointed toward a field that looked like all other fields. "There."

Broderick stepped to him, sighting down Tiger's arm. "How the hell do you know that?"

Tiger glanced at him, his big-cat eyes in his hard face steady and sure. "I just do."

Joanne came up on Tiger's other side. "I hear a lot about your famous tracking ability," she said, interested. "What exactly do you see? Or smell? How can you pick up a trail so far out?"

"I'd like to know that too," Seamus put in, his Scottish accent soft music in the dry air. "Tiger tracked me through the city, when I was in a *car*."

Tiger gave Seamus an expressionless look. "I tracked you to the car, and the car through the city. It was old, the engine falling apart, and had a distinctive smell."

Seamus exchanged a glance with Broderick. Broderick had been on that mission to track down Seamus, and Broderick still didn't know how Tiger had found him.

Joanne shot Tiger a grin. "Are you saying Broderick has a distinctive smell?"

"Yes." Tiger returned his gaze to the horizon. "And I see …" He rested three fingers on the side of his head. "Coordinates. Numbers that correlate to the scent. The numbers tell me exactly where to go."

"Interestin'," Seamus said. The lion man was rattled by that, Broderick could see, and so was Broderick.

"It *is* interesting," Joanne said. "You're unique, Tiger. I can see why Carly likes you."

Tiger gave her a puzzled look, then before Broderick's eyes, the big man blushed. Color spread across his cheek-bones and flowed down his neck. His pupils flicked to cat slits and back again.

"Yeah, he's a real sweetheart," Broderick said. "Any ideas how to follow this trail he's pointed out?"

Joanne left off purring at Tiger and brought out her phone with the map again. "Not a lot of roads out here." Her fingers worked over the screen. "We'll have to go around. But there's a housing development *here*. A long way out of any town, but people started building bedroom communities like crazy out here before the last housing crash. Good place to try."

Tiger touched the cluster of houses on the screen. "Yes. In there."

"Fine," Broderick said impatiently. "Let's go." He shouldered his way past Tiger to the truck, which inci-dentally pushed Tiger and Joanne apart.

Joanne walked absently to the pickup, studying her phone as she climbed into the passenger seat. Tiger fixed Broderick with a look before settling himself into the truck bed with Seamus.

Tiger's look had been knowing, even amused. "Don't push it, cat," Broderick snarled, then he got himself into the cab next to Joanne, closing the door as Spike took off.

THE HOUSING DEVELOPMENT JOANNE HAD FOUND LAY serene and artificial under the warm Texas sky. It had been built around a golf course, and the sign advertising the houses at its entrance said *Your own piece of the country, convenient to the city*.

Half the houses were empty, for-sale signs announcing *Price Reduced*. The people walking around the neighborhood or already out on the golf course were older, likely retired with a bit of money put by, with no need to commute to distant Austin or San Antonio.

A perfect place for a hacker to set up shop, Joanne reflected. An empty house that wasn't selling sitting among other empty houses would be a good hiding place. If the woman came and went at night, the early-rising neighbors would be fast asleep and notice nothing.

"The trouble is, all these damned houses look alike," Broderick said after they circled through a few streets. "How do humans ever find their way home?"

"We manage," Joanne said. "But I know what you mean." The developer had come up with two or three variations on the facades that mostly looked the same. There were slight differences between models, but not many. A home owners' association would be in place to make sure that the sameness never changed.

"Down there, I think," Broderick said after a time. "Yeah, that looks like it. It was the last house on a road, kind of isolated."

Spike swung the truck down the street Broderick

indicated. Joanne noticed they weren't trying to sneak up on the place, but then, why should they? The Shifters would storm the house—out of sight of the neighbors, of course. Whoever was hiding inside wouldn't have a chance of getting away. Even if the woman saw them coming and tried to flee, she'd never outrun a Shifter or be able to hide from them. Tiger, with his uncanny tracking ability, would find her in a heartbeat.

Or, the woman would already be gone, which was what Joanne suspected. Once a hacker was sussed out, she or he went to ground immediately to set up shop somewhere else.

Broderick pointed. "That's it. Pretty sure."

Spike swung the truck alongside a house at the end of the street. The road continued around in a slight curve for another twenty yards or so—the intent had obviously been to extend the road and development at some point.

The result was a street that ran behind the house, out of sight of the neighbors. Spike killed the engine. All was quiet.

The house in question was big. It rose from a slight hill—artificial, probably from fill. The land around the development was flat, flat, flat. The house was ultra modern, with straight side walls and a curved back wall that was filled with floor-to-ceiling windows. Through these, the residents could take in the great view of all the nothing behind the house. The roof of the curved wall formed a balcony for the second floor, more opportunity to gaze across to empty horizon.

Except for that feature, the house was as flat as the land, covered with false stucco and painted an earthy beige. Someone had tried to liven up the back with pots of flowers, most of which had dried up and died, no one

having bothered to water them. They were forlorn, abandoned, unloved, and Joanne's heart squeezed in pity.

The giant, undraped windows ensured that anyone
inside the house would see a pickup park behind it, and
four Shifters and a young woman pile out. There was no
movement behind the glass, however, no figure furtively
peeking through the balcony door.

A window on the basement level had been broken, the
frame and glass shattered on the grass. Broderick's gaze
went right to it, and a shudder rippled through him,
which vanished the moment after it began.

"Gone," Tiger said, staring up at the house.

Broderick nodded. "Yep. Thought she would be. Let's
check it out. Not you." He glared at Joanne as she fell
into step with him. "That woman had a gun. I'm not
risking that she still *is* in there, ready to take shots
at you."

"I'll hide," Joanne said stubbornly. "Forget it, Broderick. You need me to check out the computers. I doubt she
had time to pack them all up. She'd have run as soon as
you were out of there."

Broderick growled under his breath, but Joanne
stared him down. Shifters lower in hierarchy than the
alpha were supposed to drop their gazes when he stared
at them. They were to obey without question, to let the
alpha be their guide in all things.

Well, screw that. The alpha wasn't always right—
being tougher than everyone in the room didn't mean you
made good decisions. Joanne had never been one to do
what she was told without question. What if the person
giving the order was an idiot?

"No one is here," Tiger rumbled quietly. "It's safe."

Broderick's growling increased. Seamus started

growling now too, but not because he agreed with Broderick.

Seamus was a Shifter empath. Joanne wasn't quite certain what that meant, but she knew from becoming friends with Bree, his girlfriend, that Seamus picked up on very strong emotions from other Shifters.

Seamus didn't pick up on *every* emotion, only the ones that burst out in intense surges. Seamus reacting to Broderick meant that Broderick was seriously upset.

Joanne's annoyance evaporated as understanding took its place. Last night, Broderick had been tranqued, dragged out of Shiftertown, drugged and bound, and had fought his way free only to be shot at.

Couldn't be easy for him coming back here to the scene of where it happened. Every sight was a reminder of pain, fear, his helplessness and anger. He was Shifter, protective, and he didn't want to watch Joanne and his friends go through what he had. All the reassurance in the world wouldn't cut through that memory and his dread.

Joanne took Broderick's hand in hers. His were large, skin tough from the work he did on his house and vehicles, keeping old things repaired so his family could use them.

She stroked his blunt fingers. "I'll stay back until you give me the all-clear," she said, softening her tone. "Promise."

Broderick's growls wound down, and at the same time, so did Seamus's. Seamus turned aside, sweat on his face, his eyes tight.

Broderick squeezed Joanne's hand, his full of strength. "All right, sweetheart. I got this."

His words were merely something to say, Joanne

knew that. Broderick's eyes told her his relief that she understood his need to keep her safe.

Joanne released him. "Then what are you all waiting for? Get in there."

Broderick gripped Joanne's shoulder, the touch containing a caress. He turned from her, pushed past Tiger, who was running his hands down one side of the doorframe, and kicked in the door with his heavy boot.

CHAPTER SIX

Tiger *was* checking for alarms," Spike's dry voice came behind Broderick.

Broderick didn't acknowledge him. His heart was pounding, his head hurting until he was dizzy. Joanne understood. She'd looked at him, and she *got* him. That fact, that knowledge, was far more important to him than the Guardian Network, hackers, and even figuring out who had done this to him. Although he was still going to find them and pound them until they begged for mercy.

Broderick didn't remember the ground floor of the house—he'd been dragged through, unconscious, with a bag on his head, and he'd escaped straight through the basement window. No need to linger and admire the decor.

The echoing room inside the front door was obviously meant to be a living room. The closely spaced, tall windows rendered the curved alcove they'd seen from outside essentially a wall of glass. A lone sofa and a chair reposed in the middle of the vast tile floor, but there was no other furniture, no pictures on the walls.

An open staircase ran to the second floor, the stairs nothing but treads fixed to thin wooden strips. To Broderick, having lived in a solidly built bungalow for so long, the stairs looked flimsy and unstable.

Two-foot squares of tile in a light beige color covered the floor, adding to the beige-ness of the rest of the house. Dull. Even Broderick's house full of smelly Lupine males was much more colorful and vibrant. More so when Joanne was there.

Next to the kitchen they found the entrance to the basement. The door was highly polished wood, pretty to look at, its hinges and handle shiny brass.

It was also unlocked. Broderick yanked it open, standing aside in case an enemy lingered here, but no one appeared.

Broderick's breathing came fast as he charged down the steps. He didn't know why he was going all PTSD— he'd only been a prisoner a short time, and he'd broken his way out just fine.

Maybe it had to do with the days when humans were rounding up Shifters. Broderick and his family hadn't gone willingly. He'd lived in Wyoming, up in the mountains, where winters were harsh and neighbors were few and far between. That suited the McNaughtons, who'd existed there without being bothered for a hundred or so years. Broderick's father had moved to the American West from the north of Scotland in the middle of the nineteenth century, and Broderick and his brothers had been born in this country.

They'd all fought being rounded up. Broderick remembered the shock sticks that had kept him down while he'd been trying to get Mason, nine years old, to safety. The humans from the new Shifter Bureau were capturing cubs, taking them away for experiments.

Broderick had been kicked, chained, shocked, and still he'd been fighting when the shotgun had gone off in his dad's chest, killing the man outright.

The echo of the shot rose in Broderick's head as he entered the basement. Last night, when he'd fought to get away, his whole being, his wolf instinct, had focused on breaking free and finding his way home. Now that he had time to register the details with his human side, bile filled his stomach.

The basement was empty—free of people, anyway. It smelled empty, the only scent that of damp lint and warm computers, which had clogged the room last night.

Morning sunlight came through the basement windows, and wind did too, courtesy of the one Broderick had smashed. The sun through the dusty panes wasn't enough to illuminate the basement entirely, so Broderick flipped on a light.

Whoever the squatters had been, they'd cleared out in a hurry, though Joanne had been right that they'd leave most of the computer equipment behind. The laptops were gone, but monitors and a rack of CPUs had been left, along with boxes and cables. Plaster hung from the wall where the plate covering the telephone line had been. Looked like the woman had ripped it out of the wall when she'd scrambled to unplug everything.

The jumble looked like a pile of junk to him, but Broderick knew computer people saw things differently. They might look at *his* workshop, full of hand tools, wood shavings, and boxes of metal bits, and think it a mess too. To Broderick, his workshop, with its scents of wood and shellac, was a place of beauty, even tranquility—well,

when Mason wasn't grumbling when he couldn't get
something to go right.

Near the washing machine, Broderick found the
remnants of his clothes, and also his wallet—without the
cash but with the ID Shifters were required to carry. No
phone, though.

"Hey, Spike!" Broderick called up the stairs behind
him. "Tell Joanne she can come down."

Spike didn't answer, but soon Broderick heard
Joanne's quick tread on the stairs, the now-familiar slap
of her sneakers.

The sound instantly made Broderick feel better.
Strange that an innocuous noise like Joanne's footsteps
could have an effect on his entire body. His breathing
slowed, his muscles loosened, and the pain in his chest
eased.

"What a mess," Joanne said, the sound of her voice
completing the warmth inside him.

"Yeah, that's what I thought," Broderick answered,
not looking at her. He studied the tangle of wires, unable
to make out what went where. Black plugs filled a power
strip, with an orange light indicating the strip was still on.
"Probably we can't do anything with it."

"Oh, I wouldn't say that." Joanne's tone was light, but
Broderick heard the interest, the curiosity, the eagerness.
She moved past Broderick, bathing him in a scent of roses,
and started flipping switches. The computers began to hum.

"How does this place even have electricity?" Broderick's mouth asked while the rest of his senses enjoyed her
scent, her nearness. "Empty houses don't get hooked up
to power."

"I'm sure they diverted some." Joanne wasn't bothered by such trivial matters. Her brown eyes sparkled as she dragged a plastic chair in front of the table holding the monitors and keyboards, and she flexed her hands. "Let's see how good I really am."

The monitors flickered to life at her touch but instead of the pretty photos or icons that littered computer screens these days, there was only a black background and a few pulsing letters.

"So," Joanne said softly to the screen. "Did you encrypt everything? Or were you not worried about anyone figuring out what you were doing?"

Broderick leaned over the back of her chair as she typed. "You know, you talking to invisible people on the other end of the computer is kind of creepy."

Joanne ignored him. "You want to play, eh?" she asked, her fingers moving. A row of letters went across the monitor, then more rows, and then Joanne chuckled. "Gotcha."

"You know what the hell she's doing?" Spike asked behind him. He'd come down the stairs, and now stared, as mystified as Broderick, at the computers.

Broderick had to shake his head. Joanne glanced up at them as she rolled her shoulders, stretching them. "You know, this would be easier if you guys weren't breathing down my neck."

Broderick caressed the neck in question, but he understood.

He turned and followed Spike to do what they were good at—checking out the room, searching it for clues as to where the hacker and her goons had gone. Tiger was still upstairs with Seamus, both of them looking around. Tiger would no doubt get a bead on the bad guys and have the coordinates or whatever of where they'd gone to ground without too much trouble.

Regardless, Broderick made himself feel better turning over boxes and ripping apart the drywall to see if the villains had hidden any secrets behind it. Spike helped, the man liking destruction as much as Broderick did.

Behind him, Joanne made a noise of disappointment. "They wiped everything," she said mournfully. "That's why they left all this stuff behind. But ..." She trailed off as the keys started clicking again.

Just as she said, *Eureka!* Broderick caught a glint of something behind the loose wallboard he'd just pulled from between two studs.

He bent down to examine whatever it was, sniffing carefully, in case he was about to set off a booby trap. Any stupid wolf could jam his paw into a crevice and trip a wire that blew up the building he was in.

Broderick didn't scent anything untoward—no det cord or blasting caps, no scent of explosives or anything that would make a spark. Not even something simple like the steel of a mousetrap.

He made double sure all was clear, then he stretched his first two fingers into the crack and pulled out a round, silver disc.

"What's that?" Spike asked. Like all cats, he was instantly curious about a shiny object.

Broderick rested it on his palm. What he held was a medallion in the form of a Celtic knot. It was true silver, polished to a dull sheen, and looked very old. The symbol resembled the one on their Collars, but it was larger, thinner, and had a second circle around it, which had been carved in a delicate, scalloped pattern. The disc looked familiar — other than resembling the Collar pendant — but this wasn't from a Collar.

"No idea," Broderick said. "What did you find, Joanne?" He asked over his shoulder. "You said *Eureka*. Did you hack in, or whatever you call it?"

"No." Joanne stood up, her movements animated. "They wiped all the data from these computers, but I found evidence of where they went, or tried to go. They left a trail, a pretty cryptic one, but I found it." She sounded pleased, proud of herself. "They *were* trying to hack the Guardian Network. I knew it! Oh..." Joanne's breath touched Broderick's arm. "What did you find there?"

Broderick felt a jolt go through him as soon as Joanne said *Guardian*. The word made him realize where he'd seen this medallion before, quite often — or one just like it. His blood went cold.

"Holy fuck," he said, his voice filling with both amazement and foreboding. "I know what this is. It's a piece from the Sword of the Guardian."

JOANNE STARED AT THE INNOCUOUS SILVER DISC ON Broderick's palm. She'd seen the sword Sean, the Austin Shiftertown's Guardian, carried around, but she'd never had a chance to look at it closely.

Both Spike and Broderick were gazing at the medallion as though it would bite them any second. The two big, bad, fearsome fighters had wide eyes and rigid stances of terror.

"What are you saying?" Joanne asked them. "They had a Sword of the Guardian here? Sean's sword?"

"I didn't see a sword," Broderick said, not taking his eyes off the disc. "Not last night, and I didn't find one today. You, Spike?"

"Nope," Spike said, the curt word filled with worry.

Broderick and Spike had torn up the whole basement, Joanne saw. Pipes were exposed behind shredded drywall, and wires hung like black and red spaghetti. The floor was solid cement, though she saw where they'd gouged it. They'd have found anything hidden.

"It must have been stashed there," Broderick said. "The boards were already loose when I took them off—they made a crevice they could reach in a hurry. They grabbed the sword out of there and didn't notice the end piece had come off."

"But *how* did it come off?" Spike asked. "I thought the swords were solid pieces. They didn't have superglue in the thirteen hundreds."

"No, but they had welding," Joanne pointed out. "Or soldering. I'm not a silversmith, but I bet they knew how to stick things onto other things."

Broderick did plenty of soldering in his metalworking crafts, but he shook his head, his hand unwavering. "The swords were made by a Shifter sword smith and a Fae woman. The blade was shaped by folding and beating the silver, over and over again, but the hilt was cast as one piece." As though feeling Joanne and Spike staring at him, Broderick shrugged. "My dad used to tell me that story. He knew about forging and casting."

Joanne noted the catch in his words as he mentioned his father. Broderick rarely talked about his family—at least not his dad or even his mom. Too much pain, she'd realized.

"So, how did it come loose?" Spike repeated the question.

Broderick closed his hand over the medallion. "We're going to have to ask an expert about that. You know, a Guardian."

"Fine," Spike said, still gray about the mouth. "Let's go. Sean always has beer."

———

THE LAPTOP'S SCREEN FLICKERED WITH THE STRANGE white static that had woken Cilla Gilbourne out of a sound sleep a month before. She snatched her hands from the keyboard, her fingers hot.

"What?" she asked desperately. "What do you want?"

She'd thought she could hide out from him in this trailer in an obscure area of the city, but she'd been wrong. Cilla could hide her physical body, but she couldn't hide from the man in the code.

Her fear grew as the screen cleared the slightest bit to show the figure who'd been contacting her. She couldn't make out his face, but she knew it was a man from the way he was shaped and moved.

He was an apparition, a shadow, a flicker of pixels. And he terrified her.

Did you get him? The words hidden in code scrolled down the screen.

I tried. Cilla keyed back. *The stupid thugs I hired grabbed the wrong Shifter.*

A long pause. Cilla held her breath. Whoever was on the other side of this communication knew everything about her. He'd threatened, not only her life but that of

anyone she'd ever loved. Cilla was a loner, but even
loners had their connections to the past.

When Cilla had called him on it, insisting he couldn't
hurt her, a young man she'd known — all right, had been
in love with — had fallen sick of a mysterious illness. His
doctors, Cilla learned, suspected poison but weren't
certain.

Cilla had lost the privilege of rushing to his side, but
she'd promised the ghostly hacker anything — had
hastened to obey him. Her ex had recovered — very
suddenly — but Cilla couldn't be sure that the man
wouldn't have him poisoned again.

Why can't you use the sword yourself? he asked.

Cilla's fingers were already moving. *I tried. I don't think
the sword likes me. It wants a Guardian.*

Another hesitation, then words in code blazed across
the screen. *Of course it doesn't like you! You KILLED A
GUARDIAN!*

I didn't …

Cilla couldn't finish. The men she'd hired had shot the
Guardian dead, slaughtering a man and triumphantly
presenting Cilla with the sword. She'd thrown up for
a day.

I still have the sword, she typed. *I just need a Guardian to
use it.*

You'll never make one help you. Forget it.

I will, I will! Cilla typed frantically. *Give me a chance.*

Another pause, and the static solidified, deleting the
outline. The screen remained solid white for a long time,
then black letters and numbers streamed across it.

*I need the sword or I need access to the Guardian Network.
That is what I want. Nothing else will do.*

I know. I know. I'm working on it.

Finish SOON.

A few more characters flitted across the monitor, then the solid white static faded, leaving an empty black screen. The monitor blinked, waiting for Cilla's next command.

She stared at the computer, her chest tight, uncertain she'd truly seen the very last characters that had crossed the screen. They'd been different, a code she was sure only the military used. Cilla ran the code through her computer-like memory until she decrypted it.

The final message had read—*Help me.*

CHAPTER SEVEN

Seamus, Spike, and Broderick packed up every scrap of computer equipment in the house, loading it under Joanne's direction into the back of the truck. They covered the pile with a tarp—no use someone reporting Shifters carrying around a stack of CPUs and monitors. Joanne was mostly interested in the router box she carried, a tiny thing only a few inches square, but she said it was important.

Broderick hung on to the disc—holding it in his hand, rather than shoving it into his pocket. He wanted physical contact with it for some reason, the same way he wanted to stay next to Joanne.

Maybe living with a feral Shifter was rubbing off on him, he thought as they drove away, his fingers caressing the silver pattern. Next thing he knew, he'd be batshit crazy and have to be strapped to a bed right next to Aleck's.

Tiger was still hunting for a scent by the time they were finished filling the truck. Bleach and some other stinking chemical Broderick couldn't identify had been used to wipe the house clean, but Tiger found traces of human males in the driveway. They'd piled into a vehicle and gone away without the woman.

She had covered her tracks better, probably knowing Shifters would be after her, but it was clear she'd driven off in a car or truck that was fairly generic, he said — thousands of them out there, and likely stolen. Tiger thought he might be able to trace the men, but she would be more difficult. Of course, once they caught the thugs, they could be made to tell the Shifters where the hacker-woman might go to ground.

Tiger didn't like being stymied, Broderick could see. Tiger climbed silently into the back of the truck and hunkered down under the tarp.

They were all subdued as they rode back to Shifter-town. Joanne's pronouncement that hacker woman was trying to access the Guardian Network was bad enough, but it was the problem of the sword that caused the four Shifters disquiet.

A Sword of the Guardian never left the Guardian's side. He might ditch it a few hours if he wanted to play with his cubs or hang out with his family or hole up with his mate, but Sean kept it strapped to his back at all other times — at the fight club, traveling between Shiftertowns, checking out a problem for Liam, even going for takeout. The Guardian had to be prepared in case the sword was needed, and besides, it was a valuable Shifter artifact, which the Guardian was charged to protect.

The one concession the humans made to Shifters when they were rounded up was that every Shiftertown could have a Guardian, and that the Guardian was allowed to carry his sword around wherever he went. That had been a deal-breaker. The humans had filed the sword and Guardian under "religious practices" which was the one thing the Shifter Bureau had been anxious not to stifle.

A sword without a Guardian attached to it was wrong. What Guardian did the sword that had lost its medallion belong to? And where was the Guardian now?

None of the Shifters liked what that answer might be.

Once they reached Shiftertown, Spike drove to the house where Sean Morrissey lived with his mate, his father, his father's mate Glory, and Sean's baby son, Kenny. Spike pulled the black pickup to a halt, killing the engine and sliding out of it in one movement. Tiger got out of the back and walked without stopping to the house next door, where he would fill in Liam, the Shiftertown leader, and start tracking the thugs if Liam ordered him to. Had nothing to do with his mate waiting for him there —*oh, no*.

Joanne, typically, refused to stay in the truck, or go to Broderick's and check on her sister, or to visit Kim next door or Ellison and family across the street …

"I'm not a wilting flower," she said to Broderick as she climbed out, looking straight into his eyes as she liked to do. "Not waiting for the menfolk to come explain everything to little ole me, if they even remember to." She walked right past him and up to the porch.

Broderick growled. "Goddess save me from pushy females."

He liked that Joanne didn't take shit from anyone, but on the other hand, it was hard to protect a woman who went charging ahead before Broderick could check that the way was safe. They needed to have a talk about that.

Sean himself opened the door as Joanne reached the

porch, Broderick directly behind her. Sean's black hair was damp and his T-shirt clung to wet shoulders as though he'd just pried himself from the shower. He let them in at once, his face grim.

His mate, Andrea, sat in their large, airy kitchen with baby Kenny in a highchair, having their morning meal. It was late for breakfast for Broderick's taste, but this was a Feline family—never mind that Andrea and Glory were wolves. Felines went stealthily about all night and dropped off to sleep in the wee hours of the morning. Cats were weird.

Spike, on the other hand, was Feline, and he stayed up all night as well, but he managed to look alert and rested any time of day or night. Broderick always felt like death warmed over if he didn't go to sleep for at least some of the dark hours.

Kenny, one-and-a-half years old, watched with intelligent gray eyes as the Shifters entered his kitchen. The kid was going to be alpha all right, Broderick decided, looking at him. Also wolf.

When a Feline and Lupine mated—any Shifter crossing species—the cub was born in human form and stayed that way for a couple years, until the Shifter inside him decided it was ready to show the world his true form. Then the cub turned into either a full Feline or full Lupine. But no one knew which way the DNA had gone until then.

Kenny's gaze fixed on Broderick with a steely gray stare. No doubt. This cub would be Lupine.

Kenny's dark hair was tousled, a smear of egg around his mouth, but his eyes were unafraid, meeting Broderick's without any submission. Kenny growled low in his throat.

Broderick returned the growl. He brought his hands up and mimicked claws, letting his rumbles deepen.

Kenny's fine brows went up, and the growl stopped. The cub stared at Broderick in shock for a few seconds, then he burst out laughing. Kenny banged his spoon onto the tray of his highchair and whooped with laughter.

Yeah, this kid was going to be a force when he grew up. Poor Sean.

His mother, Andrea, who always looked sleek and well groomed no matter what the circumstance, her gray eyes a match of her son's, pointed to Broderick's raised hand. "What's that?"

Broderick, even while he was making claw fingers at Kenny, had managed to keep hold of the disc, securing it in place with his thumb. Now he lowered his hand and looked at it, but he wouldn't put the disc on the table.

"We found it at the hacker's lair," Joanne said. She sat down in the chair Andrea slid out for her. *Lair*, she'd said. Not *house* or *home*. Because she knew the hacker had stolen the house as well.

Andrea peered curiously at the medallion, then her breath caught. "Is that…?"

Sean had pushed forward. He reached for the medallion, but Broderick closed his fingers around it, loathe to give it up.

Sean shot him a glance but lifted his hand away, not taking it. "It's from a Sword of the Guardian. The hilt piece."

Sean brought up his sheathed sword, which he'd fetched while they'd paid their courtesies to Andrea, turned the sword around and showed them the tip of the hilt.

Sean's sword was the oldest Guardian sword of all. It

was the original, forged in Ireland in what was now County Kerry. The Morrisseys' ancestor was Niall O'Connor, the sword master who'd forged this one in his smithy on the wild coast of Ireland. Broderick vividly pictured the scene—the Shifter man with bare arms, banging away in the heat of his forge, the Fae woman holding her hands over the hot blade and chanting spells.

A touch jerked him to the present. Joanne looked up at him, her brows drawn together in worry, her hand resting lightly on his arm. For a moment, the two of them were transposed on the Shifter sword smith and the Fae, the brutish man and the delicate woman. Broderick smelled the hot ash and burning wood, the tang of silver, heard the whisper of spells.

The moment passed. Broderick found himself in Sean's kitchen again, Joanne watching him, Kenny studying him, his laughter gone.

Broderick shook himself. There was something unsettling about the medallion. Guardian swords had too much strange magic in them, and this piece of one likely had plenty of residual spells in it too. Broderick should give the damned thing to Sean and be done.

But he couldn't open his fingers and give it away. Something in the medallion was calling to him, as though the silver knew his name. *Protect me...*

The hilt of Sean's sword, on its end, was capped with a medallion identical to the one Broderick held. The medallion on Sean's sword was more worn, the silver polished with time. It was also definitely part of the sword —it flowed into the bronze hilt rather than being a separate piece on the end.

Seamus asked the question. "So why has it come off?

Spike had a good point—they didn't have superglue in the thirteen hundreds."

Sean laid the sword across the counter, well out of reach of his son's tiny hands. There was no guarantee that Kenny would be the next Guardian—the Goddess chose the successor in a ceremony, and she might pick a Shifter not even related to the current Guardian, who would be busy dying at this point. It was true that *most* of the time the chosen was in the Guardian's family or clan, but it didn't always happen. The Goddess did as she pleased.

When Sean turned back, his eyes held deep anger, and he looked more troubled than Broderick had ever seen him. "You all need to promise me to keep this quiet. Dad will probably have my balls on a plate for telling you, but since you found the piece—I'm thinking you need to know." He let out a breath. "A Guardian was killed. The one from the Western Montana Shiftertown. His sword has disappeared."

Shit. "Killed?" Broderick demanded at the same time Seamus and Spike were saying *son of a bitch* and *holy fuck.* "By who?'

Andrea's eyes were quiet. "Tell them the rest," she said to Sean.

"The rest?" Broderick demanded. "You mean it's not already bad enough?"

Sean gave him a thin smile, but it was gesture of sorrow, a man trying to understand a grave situation. "No Guardian has been chosen to replace him. The sword is gone, and the Guardian's body lies in state. They brought in the Guardian from the next Shiftertown over to send him to dust—and it didn't work. The body remained intact. So they had a Choosing, figuring it has to be the next Guardian who releases the previous Guardian's soul.

But nothing happened. The Goddess didn't choose. So for now, the Montana Shiftertown is Guardian-less."

A DEAD SILENCE FILLED THE ROOM.

Joanne didn't know enough about Guardians to understand why a Shiftertown not having one was bad, but from the looks on the Shifters' faces, it was dire. Even Kenny put his spoon in his mouth and held it there, watching them worriedly.

Joanne felt sorrow and anger at the Guardian's plight, but she realized this was, to the Shifters, something more than the death of a colleague.

They were shocked, stunned, horrified, even afraid. Broderick stared at Sean, his smoke gray eyes full of fury, which is how Broderick dealt with badness—he raged at it.

"How the hell did all this happen?" Broderick asked. "And why are we just hearing about it?"

"The Guardian was captured by humans and killed about a week ago," Sean said grimly. "Dad didn't want anyone to know until he investigated more. And now you've found a part of his sword."

"But why wasn't another chosen?" Broderick demanded. "The Goddess always chooses—I've seen it happen."

"So have I," Sean said, words dry. "No one knows why. Everyone involved is keeping it on the down-low— Dad asked them to. No use in anyone panicking or speculating that the Goddess has abandoned us."

Andrea put in, "Or that there is no Goddess at all, and everything about the Guardian and swords is superstition. There are Shifters out there who want to overthrow the order of things."

Broderick had told Joanne that, a couple years ago, when Andrea had first come to this Shiftertown, there had been a Shifters for Shifters movement—more specifically, Felines for Felines—which had only led to the radical Shifters being duped and nearly getting all Shifters in Austin killed or enslaved. That had been a nasty fight, Broderick had said, and he'd showed her the scars.

"Some asshole *always* wants to overthrow the order of things," Broderick growled. "But yeah, a Guardian-free Shiftertown and a Choosing that doesn't work ... I can see shit hitting fans everywhere."

"So keep it quiet," Sean said, stern.

"Like I'm going to blab Shifter tracker business all over the country." Broderick scowled at him. "Where is your dad, anyway?"

Dylan wasn't in the house—even Joanne had known that when she'd walked in. The man had presence, and the house was empty without him.

"He and Glory are out doing ..." Sean shrugged. "Whatever the overseer of South Texas Shifters and a Lupine pack leader do. He didn't give me his itinerary." Sean's tone was sharp, unusual for him.

"Well, we can guess who has the sword from Montana," Broderick said. "The little bitch with the hacking fingers. I'm still not sure how this fell off the sword she stole." He held up the medallion. "Any chance it's a fake?" Broderick's question lacked conviction. He knew it wasn't.

Sean shook his head. "It's real all right. I'm thinking

the Goddess didn't complete the Choosing because the sword was missing. Maybe she has to wait for its return."

"Like King Arthur," Joanne said.

Sean looked thoughtful, but Broderick stared at her. "King Who?"

"King Arthur of Britain," Joanne said. "There was a sword, Excalibur. Whoever pulled it from the stone was king, and only Arthur could do it. When he died, the sword was taken by the Lady of the Lake, hidden away. The legend is that she still has it, waiting for the true king to return. Presumably, she'll give Excalibur to him again."

Broderick listened, mystified. "What has that got to do with Shifters?"

"It's just a story," Joanne said. "But maybe it's the same kind of thing. You can't choose a Guardian if there's no sword for him to pick up and wield."

Sean had his arms folded, listening. "You know, Shifter historians say that the legend of Excalibur was actually about a Guardian and his sword—it got mixed into Arthur's stories in the late middle ages. The Lady of the Lake—the Goddess—decides who's the one to wield the sword. The Fae have their hand in Arthur's tales too. I've always wondered how many magic sword stories humans tell each other actually came from Shifter history…"

Broderick cleared his throat loudly, more of a snarl. "Can we get back to today? Leave this Arthur guy and his bloody sword in the middle ages. We have a problem *now*. How are we going to find this hacker woman so we can take back the sword?"

Andrea's clear voice cutting through his was like soothing rain on a hot day. "From what I know about Fae magic, I'm willing to bet that without the medallion, the sword won't do what this woman wants."

"She's trying to access the Guardian Network," Joanne said. "I found clear evidence of that. Do you think she thought the sword would help?"

"Probably," Andrea said. "I wonder if the sword shed part of itself to prevent her."

"Now they're talking about a piece of metal like it can think," Broderick said in exasperation.

"Hey." Sean pinned him with a glance. "If you'd lived with a Guardian's sword for as many years as I have — you'd *know* they can think."

"In a way, they can," Andrea broke in. "They've freed so many souls, have been wielded by so many Guardians down the generations. We still don't know what all the runes on them mean, and the runes seem to move. It's like the swords have minds of their own."

Both Broderick and Seamus took minute steps back from the sword lying on the counter. Spike remained where he was, always stoic, but even he seemed unnerved.

Joanne answered Andrea. "So, this hacker is obviously very desperate to hack into the Guardian Network. She stole a Guardian's sword — went so far as to kill him or have him killed. If the sword won't work without the medallion, I'm willing to bet she'll do anything to get the medallion back. Or anything to have a Guardian at her disposal." She looked at Sean.

Sean gave her a nod. "Ye mean set a trap for her. With me as bait."

"No," Andrea said at once. "No, Sean."

Sean and Andrea exchanged a look. Kenny chose that

moment to take his spoon out of his mouth and emit a noise that was almost a word. "Dah—"

Kenny had been named for Sean's brother who had been brutally killed by a feral Shifter years ago. Sean and Liam hadn't been able to save him, which had haunted the brothers ever since.

Sean's gaze flicked to Kenny. Offering himself as bait was dangerous, especially to a crazy-mad woman with a gun. Even Broderick had barely gotten away from her.

"Your mate is right," Broderick said, balling his hand over the medallion. "This woman is one messed-up chick who'd shoot you full of holes and pluck the sword out of your still-warm hand. Your cub doesn't need that to happen. Kenny just said *Dad*—didn't you hear him? Which meant *Don't be an idiot, Dad*." Broderick looked around at the collected Shifters. "I have the medallion. I'll offer it to her, and when she meets me to get it, we can grab her."

CHAPTER EIGHT

J oanne was immediately on her feet, her brown eyes full of fury. "Wait, Sean can't be bait, but *you* can? What makes you sure she won't fill *you* full of holes? She's already tried once."

Broderick went to her. "The difference is, I'm expendable." Joanne took a sharp breath, ready to argue, but Broderick put his hand on her lips, stilling her words. "No, I *am*. I'm not a pack leader, not a Guardian, I don't have a mate or cubs. I have three younger brothers who can step up if something happens to me. They can take care of Aunt Cora, and your sister and her mate fine. I'm just a tracker who's been a screw-up and a pain in the ass. I'm the perfect bait."

Joanne stared at him as he spoke, her soft lips parted under his fingers. Her eyes were beautiful, catching the light, even in her anger.

Broderick expected an argument to come pouring out of her mouth, or at least a scolding. Aunt Cora gave him the same look when she was about to dump rebukes on his head.

Instead, Joanne jerked away, pivoted on her heel, and marched out the back door. Broderick watched through the glass on the door's upper half as she stormed across the green in the direction of his house, sunshine dancing on her short hair.

"You're supposed to go after her," Andrea said behind him. "And have a loud argument. Joanne left so you could have it in private."

Broderick turned around to see the others regarding him with amused looks, even Kenny. The shit they'd been discussing was deadly serious, and here they were hiding laughter at Joanne being pissed off at Broderick. Joanne was generally pissed off at him, so this was nothing new.

"Let her win," Sean said. "It's the best way."

Spike and Seamus were manfully keeping their faces straight, but the two of them, mated and loving it, had decided to join in the fun at Broderick's expense. Some friends they were.

Tiger made the decision that Broderick would go after Joanne by the means of barreling back into the house from his jaunt next door, and shoving Broderick out the kitchen door with him. Tiger propelled Broderick along until they'd reached the strip of common land that stretched behind the houses.

Down the green, to the right of Sean's bungalow, was a stand of thick-trunked live oaks. In the right moments, when mists rose in that grove, the walls between Faerie and this world thinned, and Andrea's father, a shit of a warrior called Fionn, could come through. Broderick wasn't sure how it worked, but he knew Shiftertown was on a ley line, those places where magic flowed and gates could open.

Tiger moved in front of Broderick and stood like a

solid barricade. "Joanne is afraid of losing you," he said in his blunt way. "Because you are her mate."

Broderick tried to keep his temper. "I told you, I haven't mate-claimed her. I haven't even *mentioned* mating to her. Joanne has better things to do than tie herself to Shiftertown. She's made that clear."

Broderick closed his mouth, saying more than he meant to. Tiger simply listened, his golden eyes fixed.

"She is already your mate." He gestured at the air in front of Broderick's body. "I can see."

Tiger had an uncanny ability to know things that were going on with people, even at a distance, and he was usually right. Tiger claimed he'd known right away that Carly was his mate, no matter how many Shifters explained that the insta-mate thing only happened in stories.

Carly *had* become his mate. Was that because Tiger had been right all along? Or did it happen because Tiger had convinced himself of this early on and then did everything in his power to make his conviction come true?

Tiger returned his gaze to Broderick, his steady stare unnerving. How Carly put up with him, Broderick didn't know.

"I can't go after her with you in my way," Broderick pointed out. "But I'm not locking her in with the *you are my true mate whether you like it or not* garbage. It has to be her choice."

"It isn't *your* choice." Tiger held out his hand. "Give me the medallion."

"Huh?" Broderick opened his fingers, which had closed around the silver disc as he'd been hurried from Sean's house. "Why?"

"Give it to me."

Broderick shut his hand around it again. "No. I'll hang on to it. I'm going to be the one offering it to the hacker-woman."

Tiger lowered his arm, looking satisfied. "It has chosen you to be its protector. Just as you are chosen to be Joanne's mate."

Broderick swallowed uneasily. "Whatever the hell goes on in your head, big guy, it's fucked you up. Maybe when Carly brings in your cub, that will distract you from thinking up this cryptic shit. You're worse than Dylan, and that's saying something."

The mention of Carly and his impending fatherhood softened Tiger's face in a big way. His eyes lost their intensity, and he looked almost normal ... for a giant of a man with mottled red and black hair and bizarre golden eyes.

"The cub will arrive soon," Tiger said. "It will be a boy."

He sounded so certain. Carly and Tiger had an ongoing argument about the gender of the cub—Carly hadn't gone for an ultrasound, deciding she wanted to be surprised. Shifters didn't much like doctors poking at their mates while they carried cubs anyway. Carly enjoyed the arguments with Tiger, Broderick saw, so maybe it was just as well.

"Tiger, you are one crazy-ass Shifter," Broderick said, gentling his tone. "Not your fault—those researchers really messed with you. Fine. I'll go talk to Joanne. I'll even argue with her. And set it up to catch this woman before you have to stay home and be a dad. Okay?"

Tiger's gaze was shrewd, the man smarter than he let

on. Communication was Tiger's barrier to the world, not ignorance or slowness.

"Okay," he answered.

He gave Broderick a satisfied nod, then turned around and walked away, no good-byes, no parting shots or words of advice. That was Tiger.

Broderick shook his head at the encounter then jogged off into the green, where a slight fog was rising. Joanne had gone in the direction of his house, and Broderick headed there, the silver medallion comfortably warm against his palm.

BRODERICK WAS GOING TO YELL, JOANNE KNEW. HE was gearing up to bluster and swear and act like the world was dumping shit on his shoulders.

That was how Broderick argued, how he dealt with things out of his control. He was upset about being abducted—men had sneaked up behind him and knocked him out before he'd known it. He hadn't been able to stop them or defend himself. *That* was freaking him out, even more than being bound and taken away, even more than being shot.

Joanne heard him storming up behind her in the warm afternoon air. The green was unusually empty, no cubs chasing each other or adults warming themselves in the sunshine. Joanne couldn't blame the parents for keeping their cubs inside today—Broderick, one of the toughest Shifters around, had been too-easily abducted, and they were waiting until Shiftertown was safe before letting the cubs go running around again.

"Joanne," Broderick called.

At least he started with her name, not *Hey! Stop!*

Joanne turned. She folded her arms across her chest and prevented him starting his bluster by beating him to it.

"Don't you *dare* tell me you're expendable," she said heatedly. "I agree that you're a pain in the ass, but that's no reason to stand in front of a barrage of bullets so other Shifters can capture this woman and her thugs. I won't let you."

Broderick's gray eyes flickered, and he strove to mask his surprise that she'd launched into him first. "I didn't say I'd let them take me down. I only said that *if* they did, it wouldn't be the blow to Shiftertown that losing Sean would be. Or Dylan. Or Tiger. Hell, even Spike. Shifters all over would be seriously pissed off at me for letting *Spike* get killed. All that money they couldn't win on him anymore ..."

"This isn't funny!" Joanne cut across his words. "Believe it or not, some people care about you. Your aunt. Your brothers. How is Aunt Cora going to keep them in line if you're gone? And then there's *me!*"

"Aunt Cora needs to keep you in line too?" Broderick scowled as he said it, destroying his attempt at humor.

"No, you dumb-ass. I mean if something happens to you, what do *I* do? I'll have a big hole where you used to be. I'm tired of holes in my life. I don't want to lose you!" Tears began to slide from Joanne's eyes, and she brushed them away in irritation. "Just because you've decided you don't matter to anyone doesn't mean you're *right*."

She couldn't take it anymore. Joanne had been on her way to see Nancy, to check up on her, but she now wanted to get the hell out of Shiftertown and go home. Nancy was fine — she was happy taking care of her mate.

Joanne was the messed-up one—falling in love with a Shifter who couldn't see how special he was.

Joanne started walking again, but she'd make for her car instead of Broderick's house. She'd go home and sleep, erasing this exhaustion and anger. Maybe later she could function, help, give this woman payback for hurting the man she'd come to care deeply for.

"Hey." Broderick's voice had softened many degrees. His hand on Joanne's shoulder stopped her, but she didn't face him. She couldn't. "Hey, sweetheart. Wait."

Joanne refused to turn around, so he circled in front of her, laying both hands on her shoulders. His strength came to her through his touch along with the heat that made her melt every time she was around him.

Joanne had started falling in love with Broderick when he'd stood up for her against every other Shifter in Shiftertown. Because of Broderick, Joanne hadn't had to face the wrath of the Morrissey brothers. Because of Broderick, the Shifters' initial anger with Joanne had turned to sympathy and then compassion and help.

Broderick still held the medallion. Where it pressed Joanne's shoulder, she felt a tingle, as though something electric passed through it to her.

The strangeness of that flitted through her head, but it was a distraction only, because Broderick drew her close.

She felt his heart beating hard, his body flushed with warmth. Broderick's fingers were callused, his eyes hard and gray. A muscle moved in his jaw, his mouth a firm line.

"Don't kiss me," Joanne whispered, her heart aching. "Please don't."

Broderick's eyes closed for a brief moment then

opened again. In that second, she saw vast pain, deep down inside him.

But if he kissed her right now, Joanne wouldn't be able to stand it. She'd melt to him, give in like a sissy heroine with no backbone, let him take her on the ground right here.

The thought made her pulse throb and warmth flow to every part of her body. She tried to rein in her reaction. If she didn't, she'd succumb to the confused feelings inside her, the ones that made her want to throw her arms around him and never let him go.

"Fine," Broderick said, a growl in his throat. "I won't kiss you."

He pressed his hands down on her shoulders, his jaw clenched, then released her and started to walk away.

Every line of his body held anger, hurt, furious belief that he'd been right about himself in the first place.

"Damn it." Joanne ran after him, speeding on sneakers that sprang easily on the new grass. "Broderick."

He didn't stop. Joanne wrapped both her hands around his wrist and held on, but still he walked, pulling her along with him. "What?" he snapped.

"Come home with me."

Broderick's eyes narrowed. The dark gray in them turned to silver, his wolf's eyes. "Why?"

"Please. I need you to."

Broderick glanced at his house, which was quiet, the doors shut, everyone inside. Joanne saw Aunt Cora in the kitchen, working on something. Aunt Cora didn't look outside, but Joanne suspected she was fully aware of Broderick and Joanne in the yard and every move they made.

"Sweetheart, we have a maniac to catch," Broderick began, but without as much conviction.

"We can talk about how to do it at my house," Joanne said, her words tumbling out. "I have a better place to set up all the computer equipment, good stuff of my own to do some hacker tracking. Please, Broderick. Let's go home."

CHAPTER NINE

Broderick studied Joanne for a long time. She held her breath while the spring breeze touched her, and Broderick's hand clenched around the medallion, working the muscle in his tattooed forearm under Joanne's fingers.

Broderick's eyes eased back from light silver to darker gray, and he gave her a brief nod. "All right."

Without further argument, he started for her car. Joanne let go of him, but jogged to keep up. Broderick went straight to the car and opened the door, checking out that the car was safe—no kidnappers in the backseat or trunk—before he motioned her to get in. Broderick then got into the passenger seat and folded his arms, intending to radiate to the world that he was seriously pissed off.

Joanne would need the equipment they'd packed up from the hacker's place. She drove around through quiet Shiftertown streets to Sean's where the truck with all the equipment was parked. Broderick said nothing, only grunting when she explained.

Apparently, the meeting in Sean's kitchen had

dispersed after Joanne had stormed out. Seamus and Spike were a little way down the street already, walking to their respective houses, but returned when Broderick started shifting the equipment. Tiger came out from Liam's house and helped without a word, as did Sean from his own house. No one argued with Joanne, and very quickly, she and Broderick were driving out of Shifter-town, a load of computers in her backseat and trunk.

Joanne lived in west central Austin, on the north side of the river. She liked her neighborhood and the house she'd bought once she'd started working with IT departments to test system security—hacking for the side of light. It wasn't a glamorous place, just an older house, long and low, on a quiet street. She had a yard with tall trees, a lawn she paid a neighbor's kid to mow, and a view down a hill to other hills. At night, she could see the city lit up, glittering orbs of light shimmering in the darkness.

Joanne's neighbors had seen Broderick visit a time or two and no one stared as she pulled into her driveway with him in the car. If the neighbors *had* been looking today, they wouldn't have seen much, in any case. Joanne pulled into the garage, shut off the engine, and closed the door before she and Broderick started hauling computer equipment into the house.

Broderick hadn't spoken at all on the drive, and he said nothing as he carried boxes into the back bedroom Joanne had turned into an office. Joanne was now a consultant, working for clients when they hired her, returning to her office here to set up more clients and learn more about security weaknesses between gigs. With so much file sharing, online storage, and vulnerabilities out there, she never stayed unemployed for long.

"It's warm," Broderick said, breaking the silence.

"Is it?" Joanne thought the temperature just right inside. "I usually don't turn on the AC until the heat hits in May and June."

"No." Broderick set down the box in his arms and fixed her with his gray gaze. "I mean it has warmth, not like that empty house in the development out in the middle of nowhere. You *live* here. When I walk in, I know this house is all about you."

Joanne started setting out the CPUs, her heart squeezing at the regard in his voice. "I worked hard to save the money to buy it," she said quickly. "When Nancy and I moved to Austin years ago, we had nothing. But jobs were here, and we figured we'd survive. Of course, she took off and lived like a hippie for a while, and I screwed around before I figured out what I needed to do. But we made it. This house was my reward to myself for working hard."

Broderick didn't take his gaze from her. "Still not what I mean. It's not just a building to you. You fill it up, like my brothers fill up our house, but in a much better way."

Joanne shrugged as she leaned to plug in a cable. "Yeah, thanks," she said.

She straightened to find Broderick right against her back. Joanne turned around awkwardly, pinned between the edge of a table and him. She swallowed. "Yeah," she repeated.

"It's soft here," Broderick said, his voice anything but that. "Pretty. Like you."

He didn't touch her. He didn't have to. Broderick kept her in place simply looking at her. Joanne could have ducked past him, but her breath hitched, and she stayed put.

Pretty. Like you. Not many people were around to call Joanne pretty. She'd been working with IT guys a long time, and while most were just as interested in women as non-computer-geeks, they also weren't forthcoming with the compliments. They were more likely to praise a string of Joanne's code than tell her she looked nice. The last guy she'd dated had been into drawing his own X-rated Manga, starring women whose breasts were so impossibly large they'd never have been able to walk in real life. He'd asked Joanne to pose for him, thinking she'd be flattered.

"Pretty," Joanne said, her voice strangled.

Broderick's face softened. When he did that, when his bad-ass facade fell away, he was the most absolutely gorgeous man who walked the planet.

No, not a man, a Shifter—who'd taken in her sister's mate to nurse him back to health against his better judgment, and who called her pretty.

"Yeah," he said.

"I'm sorry I yelled at you." Joanne let her voice become as gentle as his. "I know you must be freaked out about what happened to you."

A bit of his ferocity returned. "You think?"

"It wasn't your fault," Joanne said. "If you didn't see or hear them, or even scent them, I bet they took you out from a long way off—maybe with a tranq rifle with a scope."

Broderick's hands balled. "Doesn't matter. I'm a sorry excuse for a tracker if I didn't realize someone had staked out the Guardian's house. Sean was just lucky they shot the wrong guy."

"Well, *Sean* should have noticed. Or Dylan — Dylan's supposed to be the smartest and scariest of all the Shifters, isn't he? Where was he?"

Broderick's fingers unclenched slightly. "You have a point. But it was more than that." A shiver went through him before he could stop it. "Waking up not knowing where I was, listening to people trying to decide what to do with me, it was like ... like being rounded up again. Only this time, it was me that was getting shot."

"Shot ..." Joanne put her hands on his arms, not liking his grim look. "She missed, thank God."

"They didn't miss my dad. Shot dead, right in front of his sons, right in front of his mate. My mother never got over it." Broderick's eyes took on a hunted look, the gray going light again. "She was never the same, though it took twenty years for her to die. She went last spring, right before I met you."

"I know." Joanne's heart felt like a solid lump. "Your aunt told me ..." Broderick had never talked about his mother, but Aunt Cora had told Joanne the story, saying she needed to know.

Broderick hadn't ever once mentioned his mother, but not because he didn't love and miss her, Joanne understood. Because he couldn't. This was a pain he kept buried, in case it rose up and consumed him.

"I know," Joanne repeated softly.

"Damn it." Broderick's voice was a whisper. He touched her face. "Jo-Jo ..."

The pet name was what did it. Joanne left her rigid stance and came at him, burying her face in his chest as she grabbed handfuls of his shirt.

Broderick smelled clean, in spite of him tearing up the

hacker's basement, though he did smell of drywall dust as well.

His arms went around her, and he let out a long, shuddering breath, as though every pain inside him came out with it.

Joanne dug her hands into his T-shirt and lifted her face to his. He didn't resist at all when she rose and pressed a kiss to his mouth.

Broderick made a low sound in his throat. His arms tightened around her, his lips unmoving for a moment. Then he met her kiss with his own, parting her mouth, sweeping his tongue inside, sealing them together.

The kiss went on for some time, heat transferring from Broderick to Joanne. She'd been cold, she realized, but now she tingled down every limb.

Broderick broke the kiss. He didn't let go of her, and she felt the Celtic knot disc pressing into her back. "No," he said. "I can't …"

"Can't kiss me?" Joanne let go of his shirt to trace his lips. "You're doing fine."

"There's this thing called mating frenzy." His voice was low, fierce. "Ever heard of it?"

"Yes." Her heart beat faster. "I've hung around Shiftertown a while."

"If you don't let go of me, if you don't run the hell away, I won't care about helping with your damn computers. Screw the Guardian, the sword, the stupid medallion, the hacker. I just want *you*."

Joanne couldn't move, as though a force other than the table behind her kept her in place. Her body thrummed with his nearness, the heat of him through his clothes, the hardness that pushed at her from the other side of his jeans.

Joanne slid her body up his, cupped his neck with one hand, and pressed a long and passionate kiss to his lips.

GODDESS, NO, NO, DON'T DO THIS TO ME. BRODERICK HAD been heating up since he walked into the place, and helping her carry all this shit hadn't calmed him down.

Joanne's lips were silken against his mouth, her breath like an afternoon breeze. Her kiss was as quiet as the house, a noiseless place, the hush unfamiliar. He was used to chaos, raucous laughter, yelling, arguing. This house was like a calm in the sea that raged around him.

Damn it.

Broderick laced one arm around Joanne and jerked her close. His mouth opened hers, lips sliding, tasting her with his tongue.

Joanne reacted by pulling herself harder against him, her abdomen brushing the ridge of his cock. She was needy, seeking.

They hadn't had sex together yet—Broderick had held himself from her, knowing mating frenzy could come upon him, that he wouldn't stop himself spilling his seed, wanting to put a cub inside her. Polite human men and even Shifters nowadays used condoms when they had a woman. Screw that. Sex was for making cubs—and for being bare inside beautiful Joanne.

Joanne wrapped one leg around his thigh. Broderick skimmed his hands up her shirt, finding the hooks of her bra, wanting her unclothed, *now*.

He was still holding the medallion. Broderick slapped it to the table behind Joanne with a ringing sound. For the first time since he'd found the damned thing it was out of his hand.

Left him free to skim Joanne's shirt upward, to find her warm, bare flesh. Joanne smiled at him when he lifted the shirt off over her head, the bra following. Her eyes were a velvet brown, so dark he felt himself falling into them.

No, he was just falling, his passion making him clumsy. Joanne laughed as they ended up on the floor, her on top of him.

Broderick cushioned her fall. A deep rubber pad covered the tile just behind him — anti-static, Joanne had explained. Broderick rolled her over onto it, coming up on his hands to brace himself above her.

"Mating frenzy means I stay with you for days if I have to," Broderick said, his voice losing clarity. "Weeks even. Until you're heavy with my cub. If you don't want that, knee me in the balls and tell me to get out."

Joanne didn't appear to hear him. Broderick had a buzzing in his ears, like a frequency trying to drown out sounds. Maybe Joanne heard it too, because she gave him a languid look and pulled him down to her.

Her breasts were a soft place to land. *To hell with it.* Tiger was right — Joanne was his *mate.*

Broderick brushed kisses to her face, her lips, her chin. He worked his way down her throat, feathering kisses as he went. At her breasts, he paused to admire them, firm and round, her nipples dark. He knew her breasts embarrassed her — too large, she said. People had made fun of her.

She had to be kidding. Those people, whoever they'd been, were assholes. Joanne's plump, full breasts beckoned his hands, his mouth, and Broderick gave in.

He inhaled her good scent, licked the tip of her nipple, drew it between his teeth. Joanne made a soft noise and arched her back, driving into his mouth.

Broderick enjoyed her taste, the glide of her nipple against his tongue, the contrast of the hardening tip with the soft of the areola. Her hands moved in his hair, then down his back, Joanne's fingers plucking at his shirt.

Broderick raised up enough to slide out of the shirt and dump it beside him. Better now that they were skin to skin.

He kissed her lips again, while she ran her fingertips down his bare back.

"Well," she asked, breathless. "What now?"

Broderick could only growl. His vision changed to his wolf one, where he saw light and shadow differently, in grays and whites. He forced himself to remain human.

"Now is me wanting you," Broderick said, his voice guttural. "Last chance, sweetheart."

Joanne lifted herself and bit his earlobe.

The world went entirely gray. Broderick felt himself fumbling open his belt, his jeans, kicking the clothes out of the way. He grabbed her jeans and ripped them open, getting rid of them and her underwear. She was still wearing her sneakers, but not for long. They made splatting sounds as they landed somewhere in the sea of tile.

Broderick made himself slow down. Joanne had not been with a Shifter before, and Shifters were big. Frenzy could make them forget to be gentle.

Joanne's relaxed smile welcomed him. Her eyes were soft, her touch light on his roasting skin.

"I can't stop," Broderick whispered. "I won't be able to go slowly."

Joanne ran her foot, still in a sock, down his calf. "I'm pretty tough."

"Not for this, you're not. But too late."

Broderick knew he couldn't make himself rise and walk away. The hum in his ears increased, like music pounding through his brain.

He realized as he slid his hand between Joanne's legs, massaging there, that what he heard was the damned medallion.

CHAPTER TEN

S tupi∂ Fae ∫wor∂ magic crap.

The piece of metal was vibrating, singing, urging him on. As though Broderick needed a piece of a sword to tell him he wanted Joanne.

Joanne was ready for him. Broderick's fingers slid easily into her heat, finding her hot and open. He withdrew his touch, positioned his aching hardness at her opening, and slid inside. The Celtic knot on the table, a symbol of love and joining, made a silver *ting* sound, as though something had been completed.

Something had completed all right. Broderick sucked in a breath, dazzled. The joy of being inside Joanne flooded all his senses. She was hot, tight, welcoming him. Joanne nibbled his jaw as her arms went around him, fingers stroking down his back.

"You feel good," she said, eyes widening. Her hips moved. "*Damn* good."

She'd thought it would hurt. Broderick saw that. Joanne was astonished it didn't, and very pleased.

"You feel good too, sweetheart," Broderick said, the

words becoming a growl. "My Joanne. *Mate.*" He'd never thought he'd say it out loud to her, but this was right, real.

Broderick held his breath and slid further inside her. Joanne groaned as she opened for him, but she wanted him, encouraging with her arms around him.

She was beauty itself, the lines of her face delicate even in the glaring light she'd flipped on over the computers. Joanne's dark curls fanned out over the darker pad, her mouth twisting as she felt him.

Broderick slowly withdrew, easing most of the way out of her, before he slid all the way back inside. Joanne's head rocked back, her *Aahhh* of pleasure sounding deep in her throat.

Broderick leaned to her, his face close to hers. "I've waited a long time for you." He inhaled her scent. "I'm not letting you go. Hang on to me."

Joanne gave a short laugh that ended in a growl. Her hands were strong on his back, her legs entwining his. "As long as it takes."

With her squeezing him like that, it wouldn't be long. "I'll love you the rest of my life. Never going to stop."

Joanne went suddenly quiet, either because she didn't know how to respond or because she was lost in a place of feeling, he didn't know. Nothing existed now but sensation, erotic and amazing.

Broderick groaned with it. Joanne was one with him, the two of them moving together. No resistance, confusion, fear, anger. Only incredible feeling, heat, need, *hunger*.

No silence, either. Broderick and Joanne let their voices ring out, no one to hear them in this house Joanne had made her home.

Broderick lost all track of time, the urgency of what

he'd come here to do — his entire life. There was nothing but him and Joanne, joined. Broderick ached where they met, the friction maddening him, but he didn't stop. No reason to stop.

Broderick sped his thrusts, and the medallion kept on singing, the entire table and all the crystals in the computers ringing with it. Broderick couldn't tell if Joanne heard it or not — she was lost in her place of joy, her body winding up for release.

Joanne came apart under him, suddenly, beautifully, her head dropping to one side, eyes closing tightly. She cried out her passion, lifting against Broderick as he thrust.

Broderick couldn't see very well anymore, his vision becoming wolf while his body stayed human. He kept loving Joanne, couldn't get enough of her. His bunched fists on the floor kept him from crushing her, his body tight as he drove into her again and again. Joanne wound down into happy moans beneath him, then rose on another wave, coming apart one more time.

After she came the third time, Joanne opened her eyes and laughed. "Best day *ever*."

Broderick's vision had gone entirely gray. He heard only the music of the medallion, felt Joanne's heat around him. His eyes cleared enough to see her lovely face, her beautiful brown gaze.

Broderick groaned, heartfelt, his head rocking back as he lost his seed inside his mate. Joanne made a hum of pleasure, wrapped her arms around him, and drew him down to her warm, inviting body.

JOANNE WOKE. SHE WAS ON THE FLOOR, THE WINDOW that gave out onto her back yard dark. The overhead light was on, glaring into her eyes.

She tried to move but couldn't. That was because a large, hard-bodied Shifter was right on top of her. Still inside her too. And sound asleep.

Broderick's head lay on her shoulder, his eyes closed, his chest rising and falling with an even breath.

Joanne realized she'd never seen his face this calm, this relaxed. Broderick was ever on edge, the protector of his family, of those he loved—the protector of all under his care, actually, no matter how crazy they drove him. Broderick had been guarding his family a long time.

His buzzed hair was starting to grow out, becoming short dark tangles against his head. Joanne resisted smoothing them, not wanting to wake him. She'd cradle Broderick in her arms and let him rest.

Joanne didn't mean to sleep again, but woke to find a blanket from her bed covering her, Broderick on his feet and moving around the computers. He hadn't bothered to dress, and for a moment, Joanne enjoyed watching his tall, nude body as he poked at buttons and bent to examine things.

Joanne sat up and wrapped her arms around her blanketed knees. "You know what you're doing?"

"No." Broderick didn't turn around. He'd taken the medallion from the table and cupped it in his hand again. "It's a bunch of plastic junk to me." He ran his fingers over the plain edge of a CPU. "No artistry."

Joanne had never thought of *Broderick* and *artistry* in the same context, but he had a point. Computers were made to be sleek and functional. The beauty was inside, both in the hardware design and the programming.

Joanne untangled herself from the blanket and climbed to her feet, groaning a little as she unfolded. Her session with Broderick had left her stiff, and sleeping on the floor hadn't helped. She wrapped the blanket around her like a sari and joined him at the table.

To be honest, the pile of computers was a sea of plastic junk to her at the moment as well. She started connecting cables, sliding conductors into slots, switching on routers.

Broderick proved to be a good help. He was strong enough to shove things around and stack them how Joanne wanted them, and put the right plugs into the right places. She tried not to extrapolate on how good he was about pushing tabs into slots, but she couldn't help it.

"What are you smiling about?" he asked, eyes narrowing.

Joanne reached up on tiptoe and kissed the corner of his mouth. Broderick's eyes lost their sharpness, and they spent a long moment in a hot, after-loving kiss.

When Joanne finally settled down on a chair in front of a laptop, Broderick paused to pull on his jeans. A little disappointing, but still he looked great in nothing but low-slung jeans and no shirt. His big hands moved as he helped her adjust the boxes on the table so she had room to work. Broderick still held the medallion, which he fidgeted with as she typed.

His body and what they'd just done was distracting, but Joanne made herself focus. She plowed through every bit of data left on the drives then traced paths to where the hacker might have moved stuff offsite. Everything left a path, no matter how hard a person tried to erase their code. A casual computer user wouldn't be able to find a trace or even be aware they could look for it, but a good programmer who could hack her way into forbidden places would know what to do.

"She was definitely trying to access the Guardian Network," Joanne announced after a time. It was coming on midnight. Her stomach growled, but as usual, Joanne couldn't be bothered with trivial matters like food when she was close to a breakthrough. "If I could get into the network myself, I could possibly figure out what she's after."

"Sean would shit a brick," Broderick said, sounding delighted by the prospect. He peered at the screen, his reflected face next to hers, and scanned the lines of code with no comprehension in his eyes. "You really know what all that means?"

Joanne kissed his cheek. "Yep."

"It's so different from what I know. I like things I can hold, can touch."

"It seems ephemeral, but it's not," Joanne said, trying to explain. "Coding is like a tool—you use it to make things work, to do what you need it to do. When I was a kid, I looked at a computer not like a mysterious box I didn't know how to work, but as something I wanted to reach inside, to unlock its secrets. I asked myself how I could use a computer to build something for me—like a game for me to play—and I started learning."

"Could you teach me?"

Joanne started at the question. Broderick's voice was gruff, but she caught the wistful note he tried to cover.

"You seriously want to learn programming?"

Broderick shrugged. "Why not? Everyone thinks I'm a dumb-ass, not much good for anything. I just fight people and give my brothers and aunt grief."

"You take care of your family," Joanne said firmly.

"You're taking care of *my* family. That's your thing, what you do. Taking care of people."

He grunted. "Sounds glamorous."

"Programming isn't easy," Joanne said. "Basic stuff isn't too bad, but as you get into it, you have to learn to think in a different way, in a different language. It's frustrating, and sometimes totally boring."

"Huh. Sounds like my whole life."

"Think about it," Joanne said. "It takes dedication."

"I have dedication, sweetheart, trust me." He studied her quietly a moment. "I just want to understand what you do."

The words were sincere, and so was the look in Broderick's gray eyes.

Joanne's heart squeezed, warmth flowing through her. "You know, I think that's the sweetest thing anyone's ever said to me."

Broderick barked a laugh. "In that case, you don't get out much."

Joanne traced the back of his hand. "I don't mind staying in."

Broderick rumbled under his breath and brushed a kiss to her neck. The caress led to another intense kiss, then Joanne took her attention reluctantly back to the screen, starting to run programs that would tell her more specifically what the hacker had been up to.

"If you get into the Guardian Network," Broderick asked after a time, "will you know what she was doing, why she wanted in? Will that help us catch her?"

"Maybe." Joanne sighed. "I don't know. I don't want to promise anything."

"Then let's get you in," Broderick said, voice brisk. "I want to find this bitch and put her out of our misery. I have more important things to do than worry about getting tranqued in the ass again."

Joanne shared his anger. She wanted to face the woman who'd dared hurt the man she was coming to love, and who'd caused another Shifter to die.

"Sean might have to give me a password," Joanne said. "If that's even how the Guardians access this thing. Maybe that's why the hacker needed the sword." She deflated. "I'm thinking Sean won't let me in, in any case. I doubt he or any other Guardian will want me poking around their databases."

If she could get in herself, without their help, however ...

Joanne's fingers prickled in anticipation, and her sense of adventure and curiosity rose. Mountain climbers got excited about attempting the next higher peak, then the highest; hackers had the same thrill when determined to break into the unbreakable. Joanne recognized the symptoms—increased heart rate, quickening breath, sweating palms, cold fingers, a smile that stretched across her face.

Broderick was watching her. Joanne flexed her hands, wriggling her fingers. "Let me try something ..."

She started typing, high with the buzz of the challenge.

Half an hour later, she sat back, tired and disgruntled. "Damn it. I should probably just call Sean."

"Will this help?" Broderick opened his hand to reveal the medallion. "It's connected to the Guardians, and the hacker killed to get it." His mouth hardened, his rage fresh.

Joanne lifted the medallion from his palm, and Broderick surprisingly didn't stop her. He kept his gaze on

Joanne as she examined the disc, turning it over in her fingers. One side of the medallion held the carved Celtic knot, surrounded by a thin, scalloped circle; the other was flat, unadorned silver.

"I don't have a slot for this," Joanne said, making her voice light. She lifted her laptop, showing Broderick the thin slits in its sides for everything but a round piece from a Guardian's sword.

Broderick shrugged. "I don't know how you would use it ... Wait ..." His gaze flicked back to the screen. "I think you're in," he said, pointing.

Joanne's hand had moved absently to the keyboard while she'd examined the medallion, but now she snapped her attention to what was happening on the monitor.

Her lines of code were dissolving. In their place rose soft green letters that took up the entire screen. The letters and symbols looked like the markings she'd seen on the hilt of Sean's sword, representing a language Joanne didn't know.

Then, as she and Broderick watched, the runes faded, and English letters took their place.

You have illegally breached the Guardian Network.

Those words vanished, and another message blossomed.

Welcome, friend.

CHAPTER ELEVEN

———————————

B roderick heard Joanne gasp. He peered at the screen but saw only Fae runes, large and pulsing. He had no clue what they said.

Joanne was staring at them, openmouthed, her eyes moving across them with perfect comprehension.

"You understand that?" Broderick asked.

"Sure." Joanne nodded, enraptured. "It's in English."

"No, it isn't." Broderick leaned forward and peered at the runes as though that would make them intelligible.

"Yes, it is." Joanne gave him a puzzled look then she switched her gaze to the medallion in her left hand. "Wait …" She set the disc on the table with a click and stared excitedly at the screen. "Now I see only runes again. You hold it, and tell me what you see."

Broderick snatched up the medallion. Nothing on the screen changed. "Nope. All I see is Fae writing. Shifters shouldn't use Fae script—I've never understood Guardians."

Joanne held her hand out for the medallion again. She didn't simply try to grab it from him, and for that Broderick was grateful. He was happy to hand it to her willingly, but something inside him was ready to fight if anyone tried to take it without his permission.

Joanne held the medallion in one hand and touched the keyboard with the other. "English again." Joanne couldn't mask her elation. "Maybe it only works if you hold it *and* are a programmer."

Broderick shook his head, not bothered. "The Guardian Network is full of bizarre magic, like the swords. It has a mind of its own. I really *don't* want to know what's in there, so it's just as well."

Joanne looked relieved, and Broderick warmed. Joanne had been worried Broderick would be upset if she could read the words and he couldn't—that the medallion had chosen *her*.

She cared about his feelings. That fact was worth more to him than whatever the hell was in the Guardians' secret files.

Joanne's fingers hovered over the keys. "Now that I'm in, I'm not sure what to ask. The secret to life?"

"Oh, Goddess, don't ask it that," Broderick said quickly. "It will tell you some cryptic shit that will have you journeying to the top of a mountain or to the middle of the ocean looking for something no one really wants found. Or dying a horrible death just as the answer hits you."

"Good point." Joanne started typing. "How about— What hacker attacks has the database has been experiencing? Where are they coming from, and what is the hacker looking for? Except I don't know how to code in this language … Oh."

"Oh… what?" Broderick came alert. "What *oh*?"

"It's translating for me." Joanne smiled happily. "What a handy network."

Broderick wiped sweat from his upper lip. "Shit, don't scare me like that. What's it saying?"

"Not much." Joanne had stopped typing. Lines of tiny Fae runes moved on the screen, scrolling upward in fits and starts. "I think it's thinking."

"Be careful what you say to it. Fae magic is tricky, and so are Guardians."

Joanne cocked her head to look at him. Her hair was tangled from their lovemaking, her eyes warm with afterglow. "You all were very upset that the Goddess didn't pick another Guardian up in Montana. Why? What happens if there isn't one?"

Broderick felt a qualm of disquiet. "I don't really know. This has never happened before. At least not in my lifetime." He lifted his hand and stroked one sleek curl on her head, unable to keep from touching her. "Every group of Shifters has to have a Guardian. In the old days, that meant each clan had their own. Even if the clan was scattered over hundreds of miles, the Guardian made the journey to send souls of dying Shifters to the Goddess. When we were rounded up, things got shaken around. Clans were split over different Shiftertowns, and now the Guardian of each Shiftertown does the ritual for everyone there, not just Shifters he's related to. Across species too, which not all Shifters are happy with."

"So what happened to the extra Guardians?" Joanne asked. "If each clan had its own Guardian, and there are now several clans in a Shiftertown, wouldn't there be more Guardians than Shiftertowns?"

"No." Broderick had never thought about it before. Mostly, he'd stayed away from Guardian business and didn't let himself have any curiosity about what they did. Sean was a friend, but Broderick never asked him any questions about the Guardian side of his life. Safer that way. "There is one Guardian and one sword for every Shiftertown. It just worked out."

"How?"

She loved the questions, did Joanne. "Hell if I know. Why don't you ask the network?" Broderick gestured at the laptop, which was still "thinking."

Joanne turned to the screen, her hair moving against Broderick's fingers. "I have the feeling it's only going to give me answers to very specific questions, and clam up if I get greedy. Like a genie who grants three wishes. You have to ask carefully."

Broderick grunted. "Shifters don't have genies, but we have a couple of trickster gods who are similar. Be careful what you wish for ..."

Joanne's eyes went soft. "You know what I wish...?"

Broderick seriously wanted to know, but at that moment, the laptop beeped. Joanne jumped and faced it, all business again. "A-ha! Gotcha, bitch."

Broderick tightened. "You found her? You know where she is?"

"You bet I do. Or rather, the network knows and told me. I've got her access logs, the codes she ran ..."

"Where is she?" Broderick surged to his feet. "I'm going to grab her and pry some answers out of her."

Joanne's cool hand on his arm brought him back down again. "I don't mean I know where she is *physically*. But I know what computer she's hacking from, how she's trying to get in, what she's looking at—and she doesn't know I know."

Her excitement made her cheeks flush, her eyes shine.

Broderick caught Joanne's elation but at the same time, didn't let himself become too hopeful. "How does that help us, exactly?"

"It helps because I can not only figure out what she's looking for but block her from finding it." Joanne's fingers began to dance on the keys. She clutched the medallion, using two fingers of that hand on the keyboard so she wouldn't have to let go. "She hasn't made it in yet, but she's close."

"Wait a sec." Broderick settled back in the chair but leaned forward to watch what Joanne did. "This hacker chick has the sword. We have only a little piece of the sword. So, why are we inside the Guardian Network and she's not?"

Joanne shrugged. Her eyes were fixed on the screen, her fingers flying, and Broderick realized she didn't care at the moment. "The network likes us?" she suggested, offhand. "It knows we're the good guys?"

Broderick scrubbed at his close-cropped hair. "All this is making my head hurt. I liked it better when I was a dumb-ass fighter."

Joanne laughed, a sparkling sound. "Broderick, you are so not a dumb-ass fighter. But based on the code she's writing, it looks like she's searching for a specific thing. Let me find out what …"

She trailed off, her focus tight on the screen, her fingers moving. Occasionally, Joanne muttered things like—"Oh, really? You thought you could hide your trail that way? You have no idea who you're up against …"

Joanne typed code, growled in frustration, or said *Ha!* in glee when she figured something out. Broderick watched her as the clock on the table moved from midnight to one a.m. to two.

Finally Joanne paused, frowning. "What's a portal?"

Broderick came alert. He'd been studying Joanne's soft shoulder and the breast her slipping blanket was baring.

"Portal?" he asked sharply.

Joanne nodded. "She's looking for anything in the database on portals. Portals to what? She can't mean computer ones—she'd already know that. Maybe places the Guardian Network leads that she can't access any other way?"

"No." Broderick was on his feet, a leaden knot in the pit of his stomach. "Shut her out. Shut her out now."

JOANNE LOOKED UP IN SURPRISE, HER FINGERS stilling. Broderick's face was gray, his eyes wide.

"What's wrong?" she asked. "If I shut her out, I won't find exactly what she's going for."

Broderick reached down and jerked Joanne's hands from the keyboard. "She means portals to Faerie. That's the kind of messed-up information the Guardians would protect."

Joanne blinked. She didn't understand much about the Fae and the mystical place they called Faerie—she only knew Shifters hated Fae for many and various reasons.

"There are already portals to Faerie, aren't there?" she asked. "Andrea visits her father through one. There are also standing stones, right? Connor told me the story about the first sword—the Fae woman came to the sword smith through the standing stones."

"Yeah, there are *known* gates," Broderick said. "The

one in Shiftertown is protected by Andrea's dad, and I doubt he'd let a human hacker woman through it. For standing stone gates, the biggest problem there is—you need standing stones. I haven't seen many of those in the middle of Texas." Broderick drew his finger and thumb down the side of his mouth. "I bet our hacker is trying to figure out how to open or build a portal to Faerie from anywhere she wants."

Joanne's eyes widened. "Is that possible?"

"If it is, the Guardians would know. They probably have conferences about it, or keep spreadsheets on it—that's the kind of crazy shit Guardians would do."

"If she succeeded, what would happen?"

Without waiting for his answer, Joanne turned back to the computer, drawing on her newest, most insidious code to block the other hacker and chase her back to whatever hole she was hiding in. Attaching a bug would shut the woman down for good.

"Who the hell knows?" Broderick shrugged, fists balled. "The Fae might come pouring through, ready to slaughter us all. They made swords that work with the Collars to torture us into obedience. Fae want Shifters to be their slaves again, to drag us back to Faerie and make us their fighting beasts." He broke off and made a scoffing sound. "They seriously need to get out more."

Joanne kept typing. "Why would a hacker want to help with that?"

"*I* don't know—maybe the Fae promised her riches and fame or eternal life or some other stupid-shit reward a human would believe. They'll use her and kill her, but she won't understand that until too late."

"Well, none of that sounds good … Oops."

Broderick leaned close, his breath hot on her neck. "You've gotta stop saying things like that. Oops, *what*?"

"She knows I'm here. She's trying to sabotage me in return." Joanne sucked in a breath. "Man, she's good."

"Don't sound so admiring."

"Can't help it. It's how you'd feel about a good fighter at the fight club. Whoa ..." Joanne jerked her fingers from the keyboard. "Pull the cables. All of them. Fast, fast, fast."

She'd already pulled the Ethernet connection out of her laptop and shut down the router, but she knew her actions were likely futile. Computers never closed down that completely until you ripped their insides out, and even then ...

Broderick was busily jerking out all the cables he'd so painstakingly plugged in. Joanne shut down all the power strips, disconnecting them, undoing any cables, everything she and Broderick had set up.

She blew out her breath when it was done, plunked down into her chair, and buried her face in her hands.

"Did you stop her?" Broderick sat down close beside her, his body warming hers.

"For now." Joanne lowered her hands, feeling a small measure of satisfaction. "And I gave her something to think about."

Broderick laced an arm around her. After the virtual world of cold numbers and symbols it was nice to lean on a warm, real person. No one could be as real as Broderick.

He flexed his hand. "I hate all this computer stuff. I need something I can punch with my fists."

"I guess you might get the chance, if she opens a gate, like you fear."

His body vibrated with his voice. "Don't even want to think about that. Fae are nasty bastards, and they fight dirty. They made Shifters so they could loose us on their enemies while they sat back and kept their hands clean. I do *not* want anything to do with those dirtbags."

Joanne snuggled against him, and Broderick put his other arm around her, enclosing her. She felt ineffectual, fighting an invisible enemy. The bug the other hacker had fired at Joanne would have destroyed everything she'd ever done if she hadn't blocked it in time — and Joanne wasn't certain she had. She'd have to wait and see.

Somehow, at this moment, none of that mattered. She had Broderick beside her, his solid strength supporting her. If Joanne never wrote another line of code in her life, she had the reality of Broderick's arms to hold her, his gruff voice to warm her, the memory of lying beneath him to bring her pure joy.

His world was so different from Joanne's. Broderick lived close to the bone, taking his comfort from his family, who were always there for each other. Joanne's world was security holes and electronics, faceless enemies at the other end of a wireless connection.

Broderick had been shunted away from the rest of humanity, but his life was more real than Joanne's ever had been.

He pressed a kiss to the top of Joanne's head. She allowed herself to get lost in the feeling, then she let out a breath of half contentment, half frustration.

"If the hacker has the sword," she began, "but it's not helping her get into the Guardian Network, why did she bother taking it with her? She could have left it at the house when she ran. She didn't need to hang on to it."

"Mmm." Another kiss. "Because a sword is a Fae

relic, which she needs to go through a gate to Faerie if she makes one."

Cold worked its way through Joanne's body. "Will it work even if a piece is missing from the sword?"

"I haven't the faintest fucking idea." Broderick shrugged, his body moving hers. "I'm learning most of this shit myself today."

"It doesn't matter." Joanne's energy for a challenge returned. "We can tell her that the sword won't work without the medallion. You were right in the first place. I offer the bait, and we take her down when she comes for it."

CHAPTER TWELVE

B roderick untangled himself from around Joanne and stood up. He studied her, sitting there all determined, the blanket tucked around her, baring her shoulders and swell of her bosom. She would never understand how impossibly sexy she was.

She still could enrage him fast, though. "No way in hell," Broderick snarled. "We came here because you were mad at me for wanting to offer myself as bait. Why do you think I'll let *you* do it?"

Joanne looked up at him, her eyes filled with resolve. "She's not going to come if she thinks a bunch of Shifters are waiting for her. If *I* offer to meet her alone …"

"*No!*" Broderick clenched his hands. "We lure her out, sure, but someplace *I* can grab hold of her and turn her upside down. She'll try to bring her thugs—so you bring yours."

Joanne made a sound of exasperation. "I didn't plan to meet her in a dark alley in the middle of the night alone. We'll set up a place she'll feel safe, somewhere very public. Like the coffeehouse I go to at the lake."

Broderick frowned. "Shifters aren't allowed there."

"Exactly. So she won't think they're there. You hide out somewhere, I'll bring her past you, and you nab her."

Joanne looked happy with this idea, ready to do battle.

"I see so many, many flaws in this plan," Broderick said.

"Yeah? You have a better one?"

"I will." Broderick put his hands under her arms and hauled her to her feet. "But later. When it's daylight. For now …"

He abruptly lifted her into his arms. Joanne let out a yelp, surprised, which was silenced by his hard kiss.

Broderick headed out of the room—she'd need a real bed this time, not the floor. Before he left, he snaked his hand back and swept up the medallion from the table.

———

THE ANSWER LAY INSIDE THAT HOUSE. CILLA STUDIED the long brick abode with its neat yard for a long time, trying to make up her mind.

Do it. Go! The crackle came from the tablet half out of her bag, words sizzling on the dark screen. It had found a way to follow her.

Inside the house was the way to do what this creature wanted her to—in theory. All Cilla had to do was commit more murder, and access to the Guardian Network would be hers. Only this time, she had to do the killing herself. She'd dismissed the guys she'd hired, had lost track of them, and now she was on her own. Just as well—they'd only been interested in money, nothing else.

Cilla had no interest in financial gain other than what

she needed to support her computer habit. She got by on very little and didn't aspire to live in penthouses and drive fancy cars. Those were useless things that bogged her down. A true hacker didn't write code to own something stupid-ass like a solid gold toilet. They did it for the beauty of the code, to be able to create something and execute it better than anyone in the world.

That was the draw. Unfortunately, the ambition to do something no one else could had been what had gotten Cilla caught.

Can I hack the Guardian Network, the most un-hackable database of all time? Every hacker knew about the Guardian Network, the ultra-secret database of the Shifters. Access was like the holy grail, the goal of every underground hacker. So far, no one had done it.

Cilla knew she could, if she had the right tools, which included a Fae artifact, like a Sword of the Guardian. As Cilla had roamed the virtual world, trying to set up a way to steal a sword, another hacker, strange and terrifying, had caught her.

He'd showed her he could have those she loved killed, and immediately, she was doing everything he said.

Now he was telling her to kill another hacker, a woman she might have been friends with in another life.

Now! There is no time!

Cilla slipped across the dark yard and around the house, hefted the crowbar she'd stolen from a junkyard, and jimmied open a window.

———

JOANNE CAME OUT OF A SOUND SLEEP TO FIND A woman over her, crowbar raised. Broderick had his arms wrapped around said woman from behind and was dangling her a few feet off the ground.

Joanne scrambled out of bed to her feet, grabbing the blanket to wrap around her. "What the fuck? Is this *her*?"

"Yep," Broderick said. "I heard her opening the window and grabbed her as she was climbing in. You might be a good hacker, sweetie, but you suck at breaking and entering in real life. Don't worry, I took the gun off her and broke into pieces."

The woman's face was familiar, triggering a memory. She had dyed black hair, skin pale from staying indoors all the time, sloppy clothes, heavy-heeled boots, and her lips bore the remnants of black lipstick. She clutched the crowbar in one hand and desperately held onto a backpack with the other.

"Do I know you?" Joanne asked, trying to remember. "Have I worked with you before?"

"At UT," the young woman said. "You tutored me."

Joanne had tutored many undergraduates as she'd gone worked on her advanced degree. "Yeah, now I remember." Joanne pictured a young, very thin girl with enormous eyes, difficulty speaking to anyone, and lots of talent. "You were really, really good. Your name ..." Memory failed her.

"Cilla Gilbourne."

"That's right. Cilla. I remember liking the name." Joanne's eyes narrowed as she looked Cilla up and down. "So, what the hell happened to you?"

Cilla's frightened look turned to one of self-admiration. "I got better than you. I've done amazing things."

"Sure, I bet you have." Looking at Cilla gave Joanne a chill. Joanne had been so much like her once, ready to commit all kinds of computer crimes just to say should could do it.

Broderick growled. "Enough with the happy reunion." He shook Cilla. "Where's the sword?"

"Safe!" she snarled. "I didn't bring it with me. I'm not that stupid."

"You came for the medallion," Joanne said. She reached for it where Broderick had laid it on the night-stand. "Well, too damn bad. I'm not going to give it to you. I've already used it to get into the Guardian Network, so thanks for leaving it behind."

Cilla's eyes filled with rage. "That should have been *me* getting in. I worked my ass of for that, *I* stole the sword, *you* just got lucky!"

"You killed a Guardian for the sword," Joanne reminded her. "I have the feeling the Guardian Network wasn't thrilled with that." Joanne was surprised how calm she sounded in spite of the shaking rage inside her. This woman had hurt Broderick, had killed another Shifter. "I didn't break in. They opened the door for me."

"Why?" Cilla shouted. "Why you?"

Broderick shook her again. "Because she's not a demented, murdering lunatic. Where is the sword?"

Cilla's face changed, her moods lightning swift. "I'll tell you if you promise to help me."

"Help you what?" Joanne demanded. "You're not in any position to negotiate. Did you think I'd help you break into the Guardian Network? Forget it."

"I have to. I have to open the way. I have to let him out."

Joanne stared, Cilla's desperation tearing out of her. "Let who out?"

Broderick growled. "You mean some fucking Fae? Hell, no."

"I don't know who. He's here." Cilla tried to reach into her backpack, but Broderick's strong arm closed around her, and she gave a cry of pain. "No, I need the tablet …"

"I'll get it." Joanne yanked open the half-zipped back-pack and drew out a tablet computer, a large one. It was off, black, blank.

Joanne touched the switch to turn it on. The usual icons came up, nothing more. "Where?"

"No." Cilla moaned. "It's different now. He's there when he wants to be. I need to find him."

"She's crazy," Broderick said with certainty. "Trust me, I've been living with crazy; I know the signs."

"Please." Cilla's imploring look was all for Joanne. "I'll show you. Let me show you."

Joanne considered. She flipped through the screens on the tablet but found nothing unusual.

Finally she let out a breath. "Take her into my office," she said to Broderick. "But I'm sitting right next to you, Cilla, and you're not touching a keyboard. You tell me where to go."

Broderick didn't want to let Cilla do anything. His eyes were tight, gray-white. He wanted to shift and kill the woman, or drag her back to Shiftertown to face retribution.

He gave Joanne a long look, then he turned and carried Cilla down the hall to the computer room.

Joanne knew Broderick did it only because he trusted her—Joanne. She understood that and acknowledged it. For a Shifter to trust a human, especially with something like this was … a gift.

Broderick did not set Cilla down gently. He jerked the crowbar from her and ripped the backpack from her shoulder, tossing both out of reach before he dumped her into the chair. He stood behind her, holding her arms so she couldn't grab something else and use it as a weapon on Joanne.

Joanne sat down next to Cilla, pretending the young woman didn't unnerve her. As she remembered more about her, she recalled thinking Cilla was brilliant but undisciplined—someone who could accomplish much but didn't have the focus to succeed.

Between then and now, Cilla had found the drive, but she'd let ambition plus smarts push her too far. Cilla had considered herself unbeatable, and as soon as a person believed that, she left herself wide open.

Broderick was a bulk of unforgiving anger. But he'd help Joanne. Joanne knew that at the moment, her presence was the only thing keeping Cilla alive.

Joanne laid the medallion next to the keyboard and rested her fingers on the keys. "Tell me," she said.

Cilla explained, in a choked voice, what to type. The code was unfamiliar to Joanne to begin with, then it veered off into even more strangeness.

Joanne heard the medallion humming, a silver sound, though not with the surge she'd felt when she'd accessed the Guardian Network. The network wasn't going to let them in this time, but Joanne had the feeling they weren't heading there. Sure enough, they swerved to another data stream, using numbers and words Joanne had never encountered.

"Here," Cilla said. "I know it's here—I *know* it."

She was scared, almost insane with it, as Broderick

had decided. Joanne stopped typing. "What are we trying to do?"

"Reach him. I'm *here*." Cilla tapped the screen as though it were a window to something beyond. "Come to me. They can help."

Joanne exchanged a glance with Broderick. He mouthed, "Crazy."

A second later, the screen filled with static, whiting out the lines of code. Within the static, Joanne thought she saw the faint outline of a man. "What the hell … ?"

Cilla bent forward and spoke to the screen. "I found them. I found the piece of sword. We can do this."

Broderick cut into her words. "Do what? Shut it down, Joanne. This is bad."

"No, wait." Joanne studied the screen. "Is that a Fae?"

She heard Broderick's growl as he started to say *Yes*, then he stopped. "I can't tell. I don't see any pointy ears."

"How does he communicate with you?" Joanne asked Cilla. "I mean, besides you yelling at the screen."

"I have to …" Cilla nudged Joanne's hands. "He won't trust you."

Joanne hesitated, then finally moved her fingers. She could watch that Cilla didn't say anything she shouldn't, stop her if she did. Risky, but they needed to know what was going on.

Cilla started sending letters, numbers, symbols. The figure didn't move. The screen filled with white again, the silhouette disappearing. The static faded, and the code came back.

Joanne watched, fascinated. She'd never seen some of the code the two were using, but she followed along.

You have the sword? All of it?

Yes, Cilla sent back. *What do I do now?*

Take it to a place no one will know. Set up the coordinates, then use the sword as I said.

Okay, Cilla answered.

"You were right," Joanne said to Broderick. "He wants to open a gate."

Broderick tightened his hold on Cilla. "Like hell I'm going to let her do that."

Something in the code caught Joanne's eye, something that made her lean close and watch carefully.

The hacker, or whoever it was behind the screen, was sending another, and hidden, message. Oddities started coming through the code, bits and pieces that had nothing to do with the ongoing conversation between the man and Cilla. She saw Cilla's lips move every time a piece showed up, she noting them too.

Put together, the message read, *Don't open. Destroy it. Great danger.* And more than once, *Help me.*

Joanne fixed a gaze on Cilla. "Did you know about this?"

Cilla looked scared. "He started sending the plea for help last night. *This* message is why I'm here, not the demand to open the portal. I don't know how to help him. I don't know what to do."

Broderick leaned between them. "We're not helping a Fae shit do anything."

Joanne didn't answer. Cilla was terrified. The young woman had been confident enough to deal with illegal hacking, theft, even letting humans murder a Shifter, but she had no idea how to help a person in trouble, or even if she should.

Cilla had come here, Joanne realized, partly to dump the burden of the decision on Joanne and Broderick. If

Cilla was out of this conversation, she could go back home to hack away to her heart's content, her conscience cleared. She would have passed off the problem to people who cared, gotten out from under the power of whoever was forcing her to help, and think herself justified.

Joanne gave Cilla a big smile, one that held a chill. "You're not going anywhere, sweet cakes. Once upon a time, I learned that everything you do comes back to bite you. Call it karma, call it the way of the universe, whatever you want. You pay for the bad things you do, no running away. And I'm going to make sure of you pay for this firestorm you've started. "

Cilla still looked scared. "You don't understand. He's hurting people—he must have someone doing things for him here. The man who's asking for help isn't the same person—he's being forced to send the messages."

"I'm getting that," Joanne said. "But it doesn't matter. We'll put a stop to everything …"

Broderick leaned to them again. "Are saying what I think you are?" he asked Joanne. "You agree with her. You *want* to open a way?"

"Yes." Joanne met his gaze. "It's the only way we can help whoever's trapped in there, and break the Fae's hold over Cilla."

Broderick stared at her for a long time, then his eyes turned white-gray. "You mean I can reach in and kill the son of a bitch."

Joanne's heart hammered, but she didn't argue. Broderick was Shifter, and he'd deal with his enemies in a Shifter's way.

Broderick gave her a grim smile. "Now, I'm liking what you're saying." He spoke quietly, which he did when he was very, very angry. The look in his eyes and tone of his voice was more frightening than all his bluster. "I'm going to take you to a special place I know, where we can finish this in private, away from your nice house. Jo-Jo, grab what you need."

JOANNE,   MYSTIFIED,   FOLLOWED   BRODERICK'S directions across Austin to a warehouse district east of the freeway. They weren't too far from Shiftertown, Joanne knew, but she'd never ventured into this part of the city.

She wasn't sure she liked venturing here now, though she doubted anyone would bother them with a large, ready-to-be-violent Shifter in her backseat.

Even in the pitch dark — it was three in the morning — Broderick guided Joanne unerringly to the rear of a smaller warehouse. All Joanne saw was the blank side of a building and a door with three concrete steps leading to it. She saw this lit by her headlights, because there wasn't any other kind of light down this row.

Broderick exited the car when Joanne pulled to a halt, and dragged Cilla out with him. He took her up to the door, pinning Cilla against the railing with one hand as he opened the door with a key.

"Come on," he called down to Joanne. "It's safe."

Cilla did not want to go inside. She was afraid Broderick was leading her into a trap, and to be honest, Joanne wasn't certain what this place was herself.

Joanne slid out of the car and locked the doors, shoving her key deep into her pocket. She ran up the short flight of stairs, following Broderick as he pulled Cilla inside. The door swung closed behind Joanne, and she stopped in stunned amazement.

The room she stood in was about forty feet by thirty, with a high ceiling, and windows near the roofline. A typical warehouse. But what filled it wasn't what Joanne expected. Wooden workbenches lined the walls, and power tools stood on stands in the middle of the room — a drill press, a wood planer, a couple of saws. Not simply giant power saws, but saws with thin blades that could do delicate work.

A refrigerator hummed in a corner next to a sink and counter with a microwave and coffeemaker, along with a couple chairs so whoever worked here could have lunch or dinner. Or breakfast if they stayed all night.

The workbenches were covered with wood shavings and metal scraps, sandpaper, and all kinds of hand tools — punches, knives, hand saws, carving tools, wood clamps, files. Sheets of metal hung from a rack, and wood planks were stacked everywhere. Over all was the clean-smelling odor of sawdust and the tinge of varnish.

Broderick hadn't been entirely accurate when he said the place would be private. His youngest brother, Mason, stood at a workbench, scowling, a small soldering iron in one hand, a screwdriver in the other.

"What the hell, Brod?" he demanded. "What does *secret* mean to you?"

"It was necessary," Broderick said without apology. "This is Cilla. She's helping us. You want coffee, Jo-Jo?"

Joanne moved to one of the tables, on which stood the product of all the tools, wood, metal, and workman-ship. She realized, as she gazed at it, that she was seeing a piece of Broderick she never knew existed.

CHAPTER THIRTEEN

B roderick busied himself with the coffee machine, not wanting to watch Joanne's reaction to what he and his brothers made in this place. Shifters weren't supposed to own any technology as advanced as coffeemakers or power saws, but Broderick always figured that what the humans didn't know wouldn't hurt them.

Joanne was leaning over the delicate stringed instrument on the table, a guitar made of koa wood. Broderick had just finished that one for a client. Or at least, it was almost finished. He had to do some final polishing.

The swell of the body rippled with the exotic wood grain, and the inlay around the edges was of black mahogany, as the client had ordered. Broderick had worked on this one for about a year. Joanne stared at it, enraptured.

Broderick couldn't move, but Mason laid down his tools and shambled over to her. Mason might be past his Transition but he still hadn't quite mastered control of his big body.

"It's got a pretty sound." Mason picked it up, tuned the strings, and plucked a few notes. A sweet, mellow tone wound through the air. A guitar's sound grew deeper and fuller-bodied as it aged, but this one was good already.

Joanne listened, her mouth open, then she looked around at the other instruments in progress—a mandolin, two more acoustic guitars, one polished bird's-eye maple electric, and a harp guitar that was for another well-paying client.

And then there was their hobby, the music boxes. In Mason's spare time, he took leftover wood, carved it intricately, and Broderick created music with brass cylinders and combs with various notes. One that caught Joanne's attention was made of onyx inlaid with gold and a tiny line of garnet around its top. Broderick couldn't remember the name of the tune it played but he liked it. Mason did research on the music, and Broderick crafted the cylinder that would play it.

Joanne took everything in then spun to face Broderick. "You *made* all this?"

Why were humans these days so astonished when a thing was made by hand? Not beaten together in a factory or downloaded from a computer? Not so long ago, everything was put together by human—and Shifter—hands.

"Yes," Broderick answered. "Who did you think did it? Little fluttery pixies?"

"But …"

"Yeah, yeah, the big badass can carve wood and build something pretty." Broderick thunked empty coffee mugs next to the coffeemaker. "How do you think we made a living before we were crammed into Shiftertowns? Or did you think we ran around in the woods hunting rabbits? Instrument making is a craft, passed down from master to apprentice for generations. My dad taught me, and his dad taught him. Now I'm teaching Mason. He doesn't suck at it."

Mason snorted, shut off the music box, and moved back to his workbench. "You didn't answer, Brod. What the hell are they doing here?"

"I needed a private place." And there was no place more private for Broderick. Not even other Shifters knew exactly where his workshop was. Most of them didn't even know he had one. He'd told Spike and then Seamus, the two he considered his friends. And Tiger.

Broderick risked much bringing Cilla and Joanne here—he knew that. But Joanne was the other half of him, he knew that as well. As for Cilla, he didn't worry about her blabbing, because he wouldn't give her the opportunity.

Joanne had moved down the bench to one of the guitars in the making, the wood bent around its frame, waiting to dry. That one was zebra wood, which would be beautiful when he finished it with French polishing. She paused at another music box Broderick and Mason had recently started. Broderick enjoyed making the innards of the boxes, getting the springs, cylinders, and gears right. The embellishments—stone inlay, lamination, and carving —which Mason was proving to be skilled at, would make the outside beautiful, but the heart of it intrigued Broderick.

Joanne studied the beaten metal, the tiny cogs that fit together to move the cylinder. Broderick had left his tools strewn all over—he never put them into a logical order like his father had insisted, but he could reach out and put his hand on any he wanted.

"These are beautiful." Joanne gazed at Broderick, eyes shining. "Why haven't you told me about all this?" She waved her hand around the room.

Mason growled from his corner. "Because, *secret.*"

"I'm showing you now," Broderick said. The coffeemaker hissed and steamed. Broderick made himself abandon it and move to her. "If you need space to work on your computer stuff, I can clear off a table. Plus there are plenty of power outlets. The building's owner is used to us working in the middle of the night, so no one ever comes to see what we're doing."

Joanne turned reluctantly away from the scraps on the table. "Any corner will do." She studied him, as though seeing him for the first time. "You know, music boxes are like computers. The bumps on the cylinders are like the holes in punch cards …"

Broderick gave her a gruff laugh. "It's nothing like it. Remember I said I liked real objects, not these soulless plastic boxes."

"Yeah," Joanne said, her eyes soft. "I remember."

He knew she was recalling what they had done after that conversation, and his mating frenzy started to rise again.

Broderick needed to touch her. He wanted the feel of her skin beneath his fingers, of her lips on his. He was also aware of Mason watching his big brother carefully, and Cilla, standing alone, uncertain, in the middle of the room.

Broderick settled for smoothing Joanne's hair. "Over there." He gestured. "Plenty of space."

On the table beside him, one of the music boxes began to play.

Broderick swung to it. This one wasn't finished, the insides laid in place and the box only roughed out, but the cylinder was playing rapidly, the music more silvery than tinny.

He realized he'd laid the medallion down next to it to touch Joanne's hair. Joanne stared at both medallion and box, her eyes wide.

"That's interesting," she said. "And kind of creepy."

"That's what Fae magic is, creepy." Broderick snatched up the medallion. The music box continued to play until he flicked the switch that stopped it. "I don't care if a Shifter made the Guardians' swords, he let a Fae touch them."

Cilla was looking around in fear but also with the first flicker of interest Broderick had seen in her. She addressed her words to Joanne. "How do you plan to open a portal and grab the guy inside without getting sucked in yourself?"

Mason jumped. "Open a portal? What?"

"No one's opening anything," Broderick said sternly. "But if whatever Fae is jerking you around tries to get through, I want him in a place I can corner him and end his Fae life. I can contain him here."

And if Broderick had to kill the bastard, he had plenty of ways of disposing of a body, hiding it so it had nothing to do with Shiftertown, no trace back to his family or other Shifters. Broderick hadn't rented this place using his actual name—he wasn't that stupid—so it was nice and untraceable. The owner knew he was a Shifter, and so did their clients, but they were cool with Shifters. Plus

Broderick wouldn't kill the Fae in a way that made it obvious a Shifter had done it.

"Do what you gotta," Broderick said to Joanne. "I'll do the rest."

Joanne gave him a look that said she wasn't sure what he had in mind and maybe didn't want to know.

Broderick closed his hand around the medallion as she turned away and started telling Cilla how to set up the computers. He knew at some point he'd have to give over the medallion, and he didn't want to. He looked at it, sitting innocuously in his palm, the Celtic knot shimmering.

He slid the medallion into his pocket. Broderick turned away and left them to it, though he watched Cilla closely. They should put a leash on her, tether her to the wall. From the looks of things, Mason agreed.

Joanne wouldn't agree, as much as she would make Cilla help them. She was too soft at heart, or maybe she still carried guilt for making Shifters the focus of police searches last year. Wallowing in guilt too long wasn't a good thing, Broderick had come to know. It made you make bad decisions. Best to suck it up that you did something wrong and move on.

Sure, 'cause that was so easy ...

He watched the two women as he finished up the coffee and poured it out. Joanne was maybe five years older than Cilla, but Cilla hung on Joanne's words as though she were some kind of guru. They busily set up the laptops and other pieces of equipment Broderick didn't understand, Joanne directing and Cilla obeying, if shakily.

Ironic that the musical instruments in this room were crafted by giants of men with huge hands, while Joanne's and Cilla's delicate fingers worked the square plastic pieces that had no beauty to them at all. Broderick liked watching Joanne's hands, and he got caught in that for a while, as they started coding, arguing as they went.

The static man didn't appear on the screen this time. He hadn't looked Fae, Broderick thought, though he'd only seen the man's outline. Fae were tall like Shifters, but they looked stretched rather than natural and they had, as Broderick had mentioned, pointed ears. Fionn, Andrea's father, was a quintessential Fae, with long white-blond hair in braids woven with beads, always in armor of some kind, weapons nearby. Fionn was, first and foremost, a warrior.

"What coordinates?" Joanne was asking.

Cilla typed, then she read off the gibberish that flowed up the screen. Must be interesting to know what that all meant.

Joanne looked up at Broderick, her expression a mixture of excitement and worry. "From what I learned from the Guardian Network, we need to create a physical prop that can represent what we need to do. Can you fashion something like a doorframe? Even a couple aluminum poles would do it."

Broderick waved at all the stuff around the room. "What do you think? I'm on it."

Easy to cut some boards to size. Broderick wasn't about to use his exotic hardwoods to make a plaything for a Fae, but he could sacrifice some less expensive boards, which he could use for something else later. *If* they weren't tainted by this experiment.

Mason came charging over. "You aren't seriously going to try to open a gateway to Faerie in our workshop, Brod. Are you insane? Or did you catch a feral disease from our houseguest?"

Broderick plucked goggles from the rack next to his table saw and slid them over his eyes. "Joanne's right. If there's someone stuck in there, we have to get him out. His message was pretty desperate."

"You believe a *Fae*?"

"I don't think he's Fae. Let me put it this way—if I were trapped inside Faerie, I'd beg and plead and scream to get out. I can't turn my back, on the off chance it's a legit cry for help."

"Are you sure that's why you're doing this?" Mason asked. "Or are you just out to impress your girlfriend so she'll go all mate frenzy with you?"

Broderick gave him a growl, but he didn't grow as belligerent as he might have a week ago. "Maybe a little bit of both. Now stand back. Sawdust in your eyes isn't pretty."

Mason glowered but ceased arguing. Broderick set a board in place on his table saw, pressed the *On* button, and slid the board through. He loved this saw. It cut smoothly through the wood and was amazingly precise.

He cut two more boards while Mason watched, then carried the three pieces back to the computers. "Here you go. Let's get this over with."

"It might not work," Cilla said darkly.

"We'll never know until we try," Joanne said. "No, *you* don't." She latched a hand around Cilla's wrist. Broderick hadn't seen the woman try to run, but Joanne must have caught the hint of it. "You started this; you're seeing it through."

"Mason, watch her," Broderick growled.

Mason, who was large and strong, stepped close to Cilla, making her more nervous than ever. But Mason would stop her, no matter what. He was not fond of humans, and if he ever found out she killed a Guardian … Best not to tell him.

Broderick held the boards in the shape of a door-frame, the crosspiece resting on the two uprights. He already felt a qualm. Doorways, even ones that looked like they went to nowhere, were dangerous. You never knew what would come through.

Joanne and Cilla had their heads together, talking, arguing, both making sounds of delight when they came up with a solution.

"I think that's it," Broderick heard Joanne say … and then he went blind.

Maybe not blind. Tiny red dots marked the room, where the emergency generators were, which, by the way, didn't start up. The computers were completely dark, no little glowing lights on the power strips.

"What happened?" Mason called out. He kept his voice steady, but Broderick, who'd taught the kid how to walk, heard his fear.

"I don't …" Joanne began, then her words were drowned by a boom of thunder. Wind howled down on the warehouse, screaming and wailing like a lost soul on a winter's night.

After a second, Broderick realized that the sounds of the storm weren't outside the warehouse in Austin. They came from *inside* the doorway he held.

Broderick ripped his hands from the doorframe, ready to let it fall to pieces. But the planks remained upright, standing by themselves, supported by nothing. The wind whipped through the opening, ice-cold, with the touch of death.

"Shit," Broderick said over the noise. "I *knew* doorways were dangerous."

There was a tinkle of metal, and abruptly all the music boxes, finished and unfinished, began to play. The cylinders spun faster and faster. The silvery music vibrated the strings of the finished guitars, and the guitar harp began to waft melodious sounds. The medallion in Broderick's pocket grew hot.

"Broderick!" Joanne yelled. "Where are you?"

Mason's shouts grew faint until they were entirely snapped off. Broderick could still hear Joanne, and the storm, and the damned music boxes, but nothing else.

Someone fell into him. Broderick recognized the crush of female against his body — Joanne, his mate.

He also realized another tricky thing at the same time. The wind was at his *back* now, not in his face, and rain slapped his skin. The scent was wrong — almost briny, and cold, as though he stood by the ocean, not in the warmth of Austin on a spring night.

He was on the wrong side of the frigging doorway. Joanne plastered herself against him, and Broderick wrapped one arm around her. The music boxes and guitars gave one last jangling tinkle and then were gone.

CHAPTER FOURTEEN

Joanne felt herself falling, but at the same time, there was solid earth under her feet. Earth, not concrete. Slippery dirt, like sand. She clung to Broderick and let herself panic.

The vibration of his voice cut through her fear. "If you think I'm going to say *It's all right, sweetheart, you stick with me, and I'll take us home*, I haven't the faintest fucking idea how to do that."

Joanne hugged him tighter, happy for the contact. "Some alpha boyfriend *you* turned out to be."

The wind was freezing. Granules, either sand or snow, stung her face. The only warmth came from, of all places, Broderick's pocket.

"The medallion!" she shouted.

"Yeah." Broderick sounded resigned. "Figures."

"What does that mean?" Joanne's heart pumped hard with fear and cold. Her short-sleeved top, jeans, and sneakers were made for warmer, softer climates.

"It's a Fae artifact, which lets you go through gates. Damn thing trapped us here."

Joanne could see nothing in the darkness, but she knew light would reveal only swirling snow or a sand-storm. Or ice. What slapped her face was needle-like, cold and grim.

Broderick gave a sudden shout, and his Collar lit up with an arc of blue. He made a choking sound.

The Collars went off only when a Shifter was fighting —fighting for real, trying to defeat an enemy. But Brod-erick wasn't fighting, he was struggling, writhing. He fell to his knees, taking Joanne down with him.

The next thing she knew, hands were prying her from Broderick. She fought, needing to keep hold of him, but his strong body slipped from her grasp.

Her hands were bound by what felt like rope, some-thing bit into her neck, and she gasped for breath. The ice-storm spun around her, the blackness becoming blacker, her lungs straining for air. In the end, she had to give up and collapse.

———

SHE WOKE IN WARMTH AND LIGHT. JOANNE TOOK A long breath, smelling a patchouli-like spice, her skin touched with pleasant heat. She must have overslept. Her dreams had taken her to the corner of a warehouse where Broderick and his brother made exquisite musical instru-ments then through a gate of boards, propelled by magic from a computer.

Crazy. She needed to stop drinking martinis before she went to bed.

Joanne opened her eyes.

She jerked, her fear flooding back. The dream was continuing.

Joanne lay on her side on a pile of folded cloths of many colors—blue, fuchsia, gold, purple, the brightest green. The makeshift bed was thick, soft, and surprisingly comfortable.

The walls surrounding her, as well as the ceiling above, were made of a purple material with wide black stripes. A tent, she assumed, but like no tent she'd ever been inside.

The place was huge, high-ceilinged, and round. The tent poles were carved black wood—ebony perhaps—inlaid with mother of pearl and silver. Low-slung wooden chairs covered with cushions and silk throws littered the room, and intricately carved tables stood beside the chairs. Her bed filled an alcove, cushions stacked behind her. Someone had taken camping to its elegant extreme.

That someone came through the door. He was tall and had the bulk of a Shifter, but his hair, which had been cut short, was pure white. Not the white of an old man—but the white-blond someone of Scandinavian extraction might have.

What Joanne noticed next—beyond the black ninja-like clothes he'd covered with a silver and black cloak—was the man's eyes.

They were dark like obsidian, impenetrable, and fixed on her. He had a hard face, sharp, his mouth a firm line. His ears, as Broderick had described, were tipped with points. Therefore, she'd either been transported into a *Star Trek* episode, or this man was a Fae.

"Where's Broderick?" she asked, trying to sound stern and unafraid.

The Fae said nothing, only watched her, his eyes never flickering.

"The Shifter I came in with," Joanne went on in a louder voice. "Where is he?"

Again, silence. Maybe the guy didn't speak English. Well, Joanne didn't speak Fae, so there it was.

The Fae approached her. Joanne scrambled to her feet. No way was she going to be flat on her back while this being came at her.

He thrust out his strong, black-gloved hand and gripped Joanne by the throat. Not squeezing, just enough to hold her still. The Fae tilted her head back and forth, examining her with his hard black gaze.

Finally he released her with a jerk, and Joanne fought to retain her balance.

"I asked you a question." She spoke slowly, though she knew he either didn't understand or didn't care. "Where is Broderick? And who the hell are you?"

The Fae swung away, the folds of his cloak brushing Joanne's body. The fabric was warm and surprisingly light. As the man moved, the silver in the cloak caught the lamplight and confused the eye before the dark part of the fabric rippled to cover it. Camouflage, Joanne realized. Fae version. Outside, in darkness and moonlight, she guessed he'd be pretty much invisible.

Thinking of that, Joanne wondered what time it was. The tent was lit by glowing lamps—electricity? oil? kerosene? Some Fae chemical?

The fact that she accepted straightaway that she'd left Austin and likely the planet Earth through a magic door and was now in a place called Faerie, spoke a lot about how far she'd come in the last year.

She didn't regret infiltrating Shiftertown though. If she hadn't, she'd have lost her sister forever and never met Broderick, a growling, pain-in-the-ass, and incredibly loving Shifter. Joanne's life would have been nothing but emptiness.

Now, her life was filled with a Fae who strode out of the tent, shouted something in a guttural language, and returned with another man in tow.

Joanne's blood went icy. The man who came inside with the Fae was ... dead.

She wasn't sure how she knew that. He stood upright, walked normally, listened to what the Fae was saying to him, turned to study Joanne with eyes that could obviously see her. He was nearly as large as Broderick, wore jeans and a T-shirt, and had a Collar around his neck. His eyes were light green, Feline eyes, and his hair was a dark golden color, brushed with black in places. A leopard, Joanne guessed.

But he was dead. Not in a zombie way—he was whole and real. But not breathing. Behind his eyes, Joanne read pain and deep fear.

"Who are you?" she blurted out.

The Shifter shook his head. "Kian brought me in to tell him what you were saying. Not to talk to you."

"But you're a Shifter." Joanne stood up straight, her mouth dry, fingers curling. "What are you doing here? What happened to you? Why are you ... ?"

"Dead?" The Shifter's lips quirked. "I was shot and killed by some humans who stole my sword. Without the sword, my soul became trapped, ripe to be enslaved by Fae who know how to do it."

Joanne sucked in a breath. "Holy shit, you're the Guardian from the Montana Shiftertown. How are you ... walking, talking?"

The Fae growled a few words, and the Shifter listened without taking his eyes from Joanne. "He doesn't want me talking to you. He wishes to know—who are you and what do you want?"

"Who am *I*? I'm Joanne Greene, a programmer from Austin. Who cares? Who the hell is *he*, where's Broderick, and why did this guy bring us here?"

The Shifter spoke in the Fae's language, and the Fae gave Joanne a mirthless smile. He said a few words, and the Shifter translated.

"Kian is a general, a bad-ass warrior who's in the middle of a campaign and looking to move up the food chain. He figures trapping a few Shifters, one a Guardian, can only help him."

"Is *he* doing all this?" Joanne demanded. "Trying to get us to break into the Guardian Network, getting you killed, manipulating Cilla to work for him?"

The Shifter watched her with his unnervingly still green eyes. "You think he's responsible for my death?"

"I don't know. Is he?"

"No idea. I'm here because another Guardian was supposed to come along and dust me with my own sword so I could fly away to the Summerland." He opened his hands. "Obviously, that didn't happen."

Kian listened, but it was clear he didn't understand a word. At Kian's barked command, the Guardian translated, and Kian growled a lot of words in return.

The Shifter looked almost amused. "He says he doesn't give a rat's ass about the Guardian Network or having humans in the human world work for him. He didn't actually say *rat's ass*, but the Fae equivalent. He's an opportunist. Grabbed me when he found me, had his soldiers grab you when you came in. He wants to learn all about where you came from and if other Shifters are available for him to enslave."

Joanne glared at Kian in indignation. "I'm not telling him that."

The Guardian shrugged. "Better pretend to cooperate so you can stay in his cushy tent. And you must help me."

He added the last in a steady voice, not betraying his desperation to the Fae, but Joanne saw it in his eyes.

"Fine," Joanne said, keeping her irritated tone. "What do you suggest?"

"Get free of this place. Find my sword. Take it to my Shiftertown, drive it into my heart. Or I'm trapped here forever."

"I can do the last three things," Joanne said. "The first one is going to be tough."

"Do it anyway."

The Guardian might be dead, but he was still formidable and compelling. The green eyes bored into hers.

"What's your name?" Joanne asked. "I can't just call you The Guardian, or Shifter Guy."

He paused a moment. "You know, I almost forgot I had a name. It doesn't seem to matter anymore. But I was called Daragh."

"Where's Broderick?" Joanne asked him. "The Shifter who was with me?"

"I don't know," Daragh answered. "I only knew he'd taken you."

Kian barked something, clearly growing tired of not knowing what they were saying. Daragh replied, and then Kian grabbed him by the neck, his fingers landing precisely on the Collar.

The Collar went off, the Guardian's already gray face went grayer still. He collapsed.

Joanne rushed forward. "Leave him alone!"

Kian shoved Joanne back with steely strength. Joanne fought but only landed on her butt on the bed.

Daragh was on his hands and knees. Kian drew his sword and touched it to Daragh's Collar, which went off again. Kian drove him backward in this way, Daragh scuttling on all fours, trying to evade the pain. Then they were out of the tent, and gone.

Joanne watched them go, her heart pounding. Had Daragh been the one begging for help through the code? He was a Guardian — he'd know how to use the Guardian Network to send the messages.

But then, Cilla had been trying to break into the network and learn to make a gate *before* she'd had Daragh killed and the sword brought to her. So she'd been working to the instructions of someone else. Who? Kian? But Kian didn't seem to know what was going on. There was much more to this than Joanne understood.

First things first. As a programmer, Joanne knew that each step had a solution, an either-or possibility. Solving one would lead to the next decision and the next. Eventually, if there were no bugs, all decisions would be made, and the program would run.

First, Joanne needed to leave the tent; next, find Broderick. If she couldn't get out of the tent, then she'd find a way to make Kian reveal where Broderick was. *If, then, else.* Simple.

Leaving the tent shouldn't be too hard. This was a tent, for crap's sake. Joanne could pull up a stake and roll out under the canvas.

She easily found a loose enough section at the base of the tent and pulled up a swath of fabric. Joanne peered through, and her heart squeezed in disappointment.

Her tent bedroom led to another room inside the tent,

this one with an open doorway that showed her more of the tent beyond. She must be in a pavilion of some sort, with many rooms inside it.

The other difficulty she saw was that plenty of Fae soldiers, armed with swords or long knives, moved in and out of the room and hall with quick efficiency. If she slithered under the canvas, they'd simply trip over her and toss her back at Kian. That is, if they didn't decide to kill her or inflict other horrors upon her.

Joanne sighed, replaced the stake—loosely, in case she truly did need to leave that way—and sat down on the bed again. Now for the *Else* part.

BRODERICK ALWAYS KNEW HE'D END UP STUCK IN A FAE cage. This one had wires that triggered his Collar if he touched them.

The Fae milling around outside the cage in what looked like a barn were soldiers. Garden-variety, working-for-a-living soldiers. They were happy from time to time to come over and stick stubby swords into the cage of a real live Shifter. Broderick put up with them poking at him a few times before he shucked his clothes and shifted to wolf.

They backed off some as Broderick snarled and snapped at them, even more when he hooked his claws around one solder's short sword and jerked it into the cage with him. *Come a little closer, shithead.*

At one point, a Fae who appeared to be a little higher in rank than the ground-pounders, ordered the cage opened and Broderick dragged out. The soldiers then proceeded to beat the living crap out of him.

Broderick clawed and bit anything he could, feeling satisfaction when a Fae snarled in pain. Eventually they tossed him back inside and locked the door.

Broderick lay on the bottom of the cage in a pool of his own blood. He couldn't understand the Fae language enough to know what they'd done with Joanne, if they even knew. These guys were at the bottom of the food chain, living weapons to be pointed at the enemy.

As Broderick concentrated on trying not to groan, he assessed his captors, but he couldn't tell if the soldiers were on a campaign or just training for one.

The animals in the barn weren't like any he'd ever seen. At first glance, they were horses, but when one of the beasts looked over a partition at him, Broderick jumped. The neck and head that turned to him was distinctly dragon, with a snout and teeth to match. Its eyes were black with a red glow from within, as though it had been created in hell.

Well, he shouldn't be so surprised. The Fae had genetically and magically engineered Shifters, so there was nothing to say they hadn't put together a bunch of other kinds of animals as well to serve their purposes. Maybe one day these dragon-horses would turn around and fight their way free of their enslavers, as the Shifters had. Would be fun to watch.

The dragon-horse that glared at Broderick, however, looked more like he regarded Broderick as a canned snack. Broderick growled at him for good measure, pretending he wasn't in a boatload of pain.

He prayed to the Goddess that Joanne wasn't in a similar cage somewhere, with the Fae treating her as bad or worse. Broderick's fear for her grated through him, strengthening him. He would live to save his mate.

He hated that they'd taken him down so easily, triggering his Collar like he'd never felt it triggered before. The swords, he thought. The ones they'd used to make Shifters obey, damn them. He'd get free, find Joanne, and do some slaying.

The soldiers, like all soldiers waiting for something to happen, were bored. After about an hour by Broderick's calculation, they dragged him out of the cage and beat on him again. Broderick refused to scream or howl, and he fought back with fervor. Another hour, another beating.

They shouldn't be so predictable, Broderick mused as he lay in the cage after the third time, in so much pain he could barely see. He closed his wolf eyes, and laid his plans.

Before the next hour was up, however, Broderick received the answer to the question of whether they were training or on campaign. The barn doors were thrown open, sunlight streaming in through thick mist.

More than a score of the dragon-horses were led in, the beasts wet with sweat, blown and exhausted. Their riders were just as weary, but every one of the Fae shits had triumph in their black eyes. Shouts and whoops sounded from the Fae who'd been waiting for them, friends greeted, some kind of beverage brought out and sloshed all over the returning soldiers, the floor, the horses. Some of the liquid even got drunk.

These Fae had been to battle, and they'd won.

A couple of the soldiers pulled Fae captives into the barn. To Broderick, the captured didn't look much different from the ones who'd caught them—the only distinction was different badges on their surcoats.

Two prisoners were dumped to the floor, then the

soldiers who'd beaten Broderick drew their short swords and hacked the unlucky Fae to death.

They took their time about it, making sure the captives screamed and begged for their lives as their blood and entrails gushed from their bodies. One prisoner rolled, struggling, until he slammed against Broderick's cage.

The look of fear the Fae turned on Broderick was terrible. The poor shit must think they were going to let Broderick tear him the rest of the way apart.

Broderick saw the thought occur to his guards, and they liked it. Gleefully, they reached out and unlatched Broderick's cage.

Broderick, in the cage, shifted to human, caught up the sword he'd captured and hidden under the dirty straw, and stabbed it between the bars and into the dying Fae soldier's heart. A clean kill. The Fae's eyes clouded, then his face relaxed into relief and death.

The victorious soldiers were not happy with Broderick at all. They cut the Fae captive apart, then turned around to try to feed the bits of him to Broderick.

But Broderick wasn't there. He took advantage of their rage, distraction, and vengeance to bang his way out of the cage they'd unlatched. Broderick used the sword to slice his way past the stragglers and then to loosen several of the tethered dragon-horses. The fresh ones spooked, just like regular horses, and started charging around, relieving their tempers by trying to bite those they ran down.

Amid the confusion, Broderick shifted to wolf, dropping the Fae sword as he went.

He had the medallion, though. He'd shoved it into his mouth before he'd shifted the first time. It rested painfully against his teeth, but no way in hell would he leave it for the Fae to find. He closed his jaws around it and ran into the bright mists.

THE BLACK-AND-SILVER CLOAKED KIAN RETURNED FOR Joanne, without the Guardian, but with a few of his personal guard. The guards yanked Joanne to her feet and half pulled, half carried her through the maze of the pavilion. They exited the tent for a mist-soaked morning, and a clearing that held a number of similar purple and black striped pavilions.

There were hundreds of Fae milling about around the tents, with more streaming in from the surrounding woods. Some rode odd-looking horses, while others marched on foot.

Not all the soldiers were upright. Some were bloody, limping, carried by others. Some were draped over the horses or pulled in on litters.

No one paid much attention to Joanne, though those soldiers Kian passed closely came to attention, well-trained.

The guards pulled Joanne quickly into another pavilion, Kian striding rapidly ahead of them. In the center of this pavilion was a solid wall, built of some kind of stone, and in this was a door, which looked to be made of copper.

A guard opened the door to reveal a long, narrow room of the same stone. Joanne realized after a second that the room was mobile—it rested on the ground now, but wheels could be attached to axles so it could be moved, like the container on a semi-truck. A mobile strong room, or a prison.

That wasn't the most surprising thing, however. The most surprising thing was a human man wearing the ragged remnants of a US Army combat uniform, who stood at the far end. Near him lay all kinds of junk — cables, ropes, metal boxes, piles of quartz, wires, and what looked like handmade paperclips.

The soldiers behind Joanne parted, and Daragh, the captured Guardian, was pulled in.

Daragh spoke, his voice ragged. "They captured him from the Fae army Kian's men just wiped out. I mean, wiped out down to the last Fae standing. The head of the leader is decorating a pole out front. Kian wants you to tell him who *this* man is, and why he was so valuable to the ex-leader of the enemy Fae."

CHAPTER FIFTEEN

B roderick had no effing clue how to get himself out of Faerie, though he figured if he built another makeshift door and shoved the medallion from the Guardian's sword at it, that might work. He might end up in downtown Chicago, stark naked, but oh well. At least he'd be out of this place.

But like hell he was going to try without Joanne. He'd find her and take her the fuck home. Then mate with her, let the frenzy take him, and drag Liam out of his house to perform the sun and moon ceremonies. Then they'd be together always.

First, Broderick had to find her. He'd kill every single one of the Fae if they'd touched her. Hell, he might just kill them anyway.

Broderick took cover in a stand of tall forest that seemed to be everywhere. The clearing in the middle was full of tents, though the barn looked like a permanent structure—likely the army had kicked out a hapless Fae farmer and taken it over.

The tents were made of what looked like canvas, most

striped in a black and purple design, and each had pennants flying at the entrances and from the top. The pennants didn't flap much in the still air, but he could make out that they were blue with a gold dragon emblem.

The tents all looked alike, but he figured the leader stayed in the one with the most guards. At least the guy wasn't stupid enough to make his tent more lavishly decorated and obvious from the others. Anyone with a good projectile weapon would know which one to take out.

In front of this compound of tents, soldiers were erecting a wide pole with a spear lashed to its top. A couple Fae climbed this, then the ones below handed something up with great delight. A Fae at the top smashed the object onto the spear.

A head, Broderick realized. Bile rose in his throat. Stupid Fae dickheads. Shifters honored their dead, even that of their enemies, sending them off with dignity. The Fae, who'd been barbaric for centuries, defiled everything they touched. They had no compassion inside them, only brutality.

Broderick settled in between the trees and waited. Feline Shifters might brag about what great stalkers they were and how long they could lie still, but Broderick was going to give them a run for their money. Wolves had infinite patience. Broderick was also willing to bet the Felines simply fell asleep and woke up when something interesting happened.

On the other hand, Broderick was itching to charge, kill, tear down the fancy tents and dig through their shreds until he found Joanne. *If* she was even there.

She was. The entrance to the head honcho's tent opened, and out came a guy dressed all in black and silver. Two guards had Joanne between them and they pulled her along behind the black-and-silver guy.

Joanne looked all right. She wasn't covered in blood or contusions, or staggering, limp and defeated. She struggled even now, giving her captors a fiery look. Good for her. Now to get her away from them.

Broderick calculated that if he charged, he'd make it about a hundred feet before he was shot full of arrows or slashed apart with swords. The field was flowing with soldiers, and more joined them every minute.

Stealth it was, then.

Broderick chose his target and slunk toward it on his belly across mud and dead leaves. He hated the stink — it would take him days to wash the smell of Fae from his fur.

The soldier watching the perimeter was disgruntled, Broderick could tell, having to stand guard while his friends celebrated by cutting more captives to bits and splashing each other with their blood. Fae were sick bastards.

Broderick paused to shift to human before he made his final approach, not trusting himself to be able to change quickly enough when he got closer.

The Fae soldier never heard him coming. Broderick had his arm around the man's neck in a chokehold before he could react. The Fae's halfhearted shout became a gurgle, the guy struggling for breath. Broderick smacked him hard in the temple with his solid hand, and the Fae went down in a tangle of limbs.

Broderick had chosen this particular soldier because he was large. Broderick wasn't thrilled with the Fae fashion of leggings, surcoats, and chainmail, but he planned to steal one of the dragon-horses and didn't want to ride it bare-assed.

He dragged the guy out of sight, stripped him, and pulled on the clothes. They were made of a light gray and black fabric which rested easily against Broderick's skin. The leggings were a little too tight, and the tunic tore, but what the hell. Broderick also took all the Fae's weapons, buckling them around his torso.

He skulked along for a while, the gray and black coloring of the clothes helping him hide in shadows and mists. Many of the dragon-horses were tired or injured, coming in from the battle. Those wouldn't help him. Broderick needed a horse that had been held in reserve, one with plenty of energy.

That meant that the crazy dragon thing would try to fight him. Oh, well. For years Broderick had managed to keep in line three seriously angry wolf Shifter males who barely acknowledged that their oldest brother was their alpha. Taming a horse that could slash Broderick to bits would be a picnic in comparison.

He kept to the shadows of a large tree with feathery growths hanging from it. Those stunk too. Goddess, how could the Fae stand this place?

A soldier came out with a horse that was nearly dancing on its cloven hooves. The Fae dressed light for riding, with no armor and only a short sword. A messenger of some kind, Broderick deduced.

The horse was keyed up from the excitement and probably wanted to stay with its friends to party just like the soldiers did. The Fae guy cursed—Broderick understood the gist if he didn't know the words. The Fae turned the horse in a circle, trying to calm it.

The horse reached out with its sharp canines and ripped the Fae's tunic from his shoulder. The man snarled, smacked the horse in the side, and the horse attacked him.

Broderick was out from under his cover, running for them. The Fae saw him, mistook him for another soldier coming to help, and opened his mouth to shout. Then the Fae's eyes widened, shock on his face, as he registered that Broderick was no Fae. The horse took advantage of the Fae's distraction to try to tear off half his arm.

The Fae screamed, the scream cutting short when Broderick clamped his hand around the man's mouth. A smash with the butt of one of the handy knives had the Fae on the ground.

The horse, loose, went insane. It tried to trample the soldier — Broderick shoved the horse until its hooves landed on dirt and leaves, and rolled the Fae back under the cover of the trees.

The dragon head then came at Broderick, fire in the beast's eyes. Mason looked kind of like that if you woke him up too early.

The dragon-horse went for Broderick with its teeth. Broderick ducked, grabbed the leathery tendrils of its mane, and launched himself onto the dragon-horse's back.

The creature danced around, bucking and twisting. Broderick held on grimly, lowering himself to wrap his arms around the thing. If there were a rodeo event with one of these demons, Broderick would be on his way to bagging a trophy for it.

Broderick's hand brushed the medallion he'd thrust into the pocket of the leggings. Still clinging to the horse, he worked the disc out with his fingers, needing to hold it for some reason, even now, of all times.

Once the medallion was in his palm, he pressed it to

the horse's side. The horse reared and bucked, screaming, then suddenly it settled down, shying sideways and trembling.

"That's more like it," Broderick growled. Keeping the medallion in his hand, he turned the horse with his legs and its mane, and rode off into the woods.

———

JOANNE BLINKED AT THE MAN WHO FACED HER. HE wasn't much older than she was—late twenties, early thirties at most—though his face held the grim lines of someone who'd seen the hard side of life. His uniform was desert camouflage, ragged, his name tag torn off. He had stripes on his sleeve, but Joanne wasn't familiar enough with rank insignia to know what they meant. A sergeant of some kind, she assumed. The tag that remained read "U.S. Army."

The man stared back at her in suspicion. That she was a fellow prisoner, there could be no doubt, but he wasn't going to trust her blindly. Joanne didn't blame him—he'd likely been through too much to easily trust.

"Who are you?" she asked. She glanced at Kian. "He can't understand us."

"Who are *you*?" the man countered. His accent was Southern though not Texas.

"My name's Joanne. I'm from Austin. I got caught when I stumbled in here ..." Her gaze went to the makeshift equipment, the wires, clamps he'd shaped from the wires, pieces of clear quartz. "Were you trying to build a radio from crystals?" She went down on her knees to look at it all in wonder.

"What do you know about it?" the man demanded.

"Not a lot," Joanne admitted. "I used to read about this stuff when I was younger — I wanted to know everything I could about electronics. Where do you get electricity to run it?"

The man's eyes were blue, his hair sand color, as were his eyelashes. He studied her for a time before he answered. "The other Fae, the one who caught me before this bunch slaughtered him, had a small generator. Used friction, usually from enslaved people pumping it. But enough to spark a battery and run a signal."

"Why?" Joanne touched one of the quartz crystals, then she snapped her gaze back to the man. She thought about the signal she'd seen on her computer screen, and the outline of a man in the static. "You're the guy in the computer! I mean — the one sending messages in the code. Right? You did it with *this*?"

"I sent pulses." He shot a glance at the Guardian, who was watching them, Kian's big hand on his shoulder. "Are you going to tell him all this?" he asked Daragh.

"Only what he needs to know," Daragh said. He switched to the Fae language and began to talk.

Kian grunted a few times, his shrewd eyes running over the man and Joanne.

"He wants you to build it again," Daragh said. "Whatever it is."

"We'd better do it," Joanne said. "I'll help you. If Cilla is still out there, waiting for you to send another signal, she might be able to do something to help us."

"Cilla? Is that her name?" The young man gave Joanne a half smile, which made his face suddenly handsome. "I only knew her as wildkitty287."

"Oh, she has a name, all right," Joanne said. "Plus

she's out of control. Don't get any warm fuzzies about her."

"She was scared," the young man said. "Desperate. Caught. Like me." He started laying out the crystals and wires against the electronics board he pulled out of his pack, something he'd obviously brought into Faerie with him. "The Fae who captured me was trying to open a way to our world wherever he wanted, not just on ley lines. He planned to lead his army across, grab Shifters, and take over. Short-sighted, but what do you do with guys like that? He made me send the messages. So, thank this Fae here for stopping him." He jerked his chin at Kian.

Joanne glanced at Kian, who'd folded his arms and settled in to watch. "What's to say he won't try the same thing?"

"He's not interested," Daragh said. "I haven't studied him long, but he's all about power *within* Faerie. The other Fae took up territory he wanted. So Kian stole it and wiped the other faction out. Fae logic."

"Hmm," Joanne said. She looked up at Daragh. "Why does Kian want this radio to work then?"

The Guardian and Kian exchanged a few phrases. "Anything to help him in his conquest," Daragh said. "If he can't use it, he'll destroy it."

"Good to know," Joanne said. At least, with the other Fae dead, Cilla would be free of the threat to her friends … well, if whoever worked for the defeated Fae didn't take his revenge on Cilla. Joanne would have to alert Dylan, if they could get back. "We won't have long to contact Cilla, I'm thinking," Joanne said to the man. "If we even can."

He flashed her a resigned look. "Hand me that clamp.

My name's Remy, by the way. Fayette. Staff Sergeant. Didn't mean to be rude."

Joanne hid her start by dropping a set of wires and scooping them up again. She said casually, pretending to ask him a question about what went where, "You're Bree's brother."

His eyes widened slightly, and he looked down so Kian wouldn't notice his expression. "Now how the hell did you know that?" The Southern accent deepened.

"I know Bree. She lives in Austin now. She thinks you died when your helicopter was shot down in Afghanistan."

"I should have," Remy Fayette said as he bent over the board. "I really should have. Is she all right? And my mom?"

"They're both great. They're in Austin now. Bree's living with a Shifter. Your mom lives in your great-uncle's house."

"Man." Remy's eyes opened and closed, moisture on his lashes. "You get shot at and dragged into Faerie for a few months, and look what happens?"

"We'll have a big party when we get back. Now, let's build us a computer out of scraps."

"Sure," Remy said. "How are we going to power it?"

"Heck if I know." Joanne helped him twist wires into holes. "I'll think of something. If I can hack the Guardian Network, I can hack a bunch of quartz crystals."

Daragh growled when Joanne mentioned the Guardian Network, but he said nothing.

Kian got up and came over to watch what they were doing. He pointed and asked a question. Daragh translated, but there wasn't much need. "What does that do?"

Remy explained. "It can send and receive signals over long distances. If there are signals to receive."

Kian followed Daragh's translation with interest. He reached down and touched a crystal, then snatched his finger back as though worried it would bite him.

"Signals are all over our world," Joanne said. "All kinds of waves. Why shouldn't there be some here as well?"

"There are," Remy said. "Different ones. I'm in the signal corps—communications was kind of my raison d'être. There's plenty of stuff in the atmosphere here too. Faerie's an alternate world to ours—like what would happen if the timeline had veered off centuries ago—not a different planet. Near as I can figure, anyway."

"Which is why we can pass back and forth on ley lines and through magic doors," Joanne said, thinking it through. "Worlds running almost in sync, then growing more dissimilar with the passing years. Huh. Will give me something to think about in the middle of the night when I'm back home."

"Yeah, me too."

"We still need electricity," Joanne said. She looked up at Daragh, a muscular Shifter in T-shirt and stained jeans and motorcycle boots. "There's power in your Collar," she said. "If you're no longer truly alive, can't you take it off?"

"Now, there's an idea." Daragh gave her a wry look. "I might be dead, but it still hurts like hell. As you saw." He put his hand to his throat. "I tried. I can't get it off, no matter what I do." He glanced at Kian, who was tracing the wires and clips with his gaze, as though memorizing the pattern. "How about if I piss him off? I'm sure he'd be happy to trigger my Collar for you."

"No," Joanne said quickly. She already knew in her heart she couldn't help Daragh—not to save his life anyway. But she refused to stand there and watch him be tortured on the off chance it would send a signal to their side of the ether.

Remy said, "Without power, this will be just a pretty collection of rocks and wires. I can try to make a battery. Got any salt water?"

Joanne was about to answer when the walls shook, shouting sounded, and smoke poured through the doorway into the stone room. Joanne coughed. Remy caught her and dove for the ground, pushing her underneath him.

Kian disappeared into the boiling smoke, his sword making a ringing sound as he drew it. Daragh, unaffected, walked calmly to the door and out. Kian wasn't far behind him, and then the room moved. The Fae were going to try to make it mobile.

Joanne struggled out from under Remy and was up, running for the door, left open, Remy right behind her. Soldiers were everywhere, yelling, silhouettes in the smoke.

Joanne heard the scream of a horse, hoofbeats, and then a demon-creature was charging through a slit in one of the canvas walls, right through the smoke and fire.

The beast was a horse—at least, half of it was. Its neck and head were sinuous, covered with scales. Its eyes were red, its teeth sharp points in a wide, dragon-like mouth.

On its back was Broderick, dressed like a Fae.

Broderick rode straight at her, like a knight in shining armor, grabbed Joanne by the arm, and hauled her up onto the horse in front of him.

CHAPTER SIXTEEN

W ait!" Joanne yelled as Broderick turned the dragon-horse and prepared to charge back out through the tent wall. "We can't go without Remy. And his radio—we need that!"

"What?" Broderick shouted back. Having the weight of Joanne against him was all he needed. "No *Oh, Broderick, my hero!* Or even *How the hell did you find me?* Who is Remy, and why do I care?"

"He's Bree's brother, and he has a way to get us out of here."

Broderick growled even as he turned the horse. "Damn it, I knew this couldn't be that easy."

He rode through the smoke at the wall with the copper door, as a man in an army uniform carrying armfuls of junk came out. Joanne slid down before Broderick could stop her and went to help him. How Joanne expected Broderick to take the man and all the stuff, and Joanne, somewhere safe he had no idea.

Broderick smothered more astonishment when another man bulked through the smoke.

He was a Shifter. He had the build, the take-no-shit green eyes of a Feline, the attitude. Broderick would have known he was Shifter even before he saw the Collar.

The Shifter was too pale to be healthy, and his eyes were haunted. He met Broderick's gaze with a skewering stare—an alpha.

"Who the fuck are you?" Broderick demanded with his usual directness.

The Shifter carried lightweight packs, which he tossed at Remy and Joanne. Without question, the two started stuffing the equipment into them.

"Daragh O'Sullivan," the Shifter answered. "Guardian. Dead. Long story."

"You didn't get dusted," Broderick said, dread and amazement creeping through him. This was the Guardian who'd been killed, whose body still lay in state up in Montana. "Crap on a crutch, your soul got trapped."

"Yep." Daragh gave Broderick a slow nod. The stoic acceptance of his fate only made Broderick shudder again. "I'd appreciate it if you located my sword and drove it through my heart."

Or he'd be here for eternity, Broderick knew. He saw the horror of that in Daragh's eyes. The Fae not only wanted to enslave Shifter bodies but their souls as well.

"You got it," Broderick said. "Joanne, we need to move."

"Stop yelling." Joanne came running, a clinking bag over her shoulder. "What is that thing?" She pointed to the horse.

"Transportation." He yanked the dragon-horse's head aside as it tried to bite Joanne. Broderick hauled Joanne onto its back with him, the bag swinging.

Remy came after her, and Daragh helped boost Remy

up behind Broderick. The horse danced but was strong enough to carry them all. As long as Broderick could keep it under control, all would be well.

Remy held on to Broderick from behind, and Broderick held Joanne, a much nicer armful. He turned the dragon-horse and charged back out, through the tent and the soldiers and the smoke from the fires he'd lit. The raw alcohol of the soldiers' celebratory drink, which they carried in highly pressurized bottles, had made nice explosives.

Broderick made for the woods. The only way he could see getting out of this was to keep ahead of the Fae long enough to let Joanne and her new friend work out a way to take them home, if they could.

"Why didn't we bring the other guy?" Remy yelled as they charged through the camp. "He's a prisoner too, right?"

"He's not really here," Broderick called back. "The only way we free him is if we get home. What about you? Bree's brother, eh? Don't tell me you're dead too."

"I don't think so," Remy said, his accent like Bree's. "I saw the missile coming at the helicopter ... and then I was here. I was captured in like, three seconds. Fell right into the path of some seriously crazy dudes."

"That's what Fae are. Seriously crazy dudes ... Aw, *shit*."

Broderick swerved the horse, but a dozen Fae had risen from among the thick scrub in the woods, arrows nocked. They didn't bother to warn Broderick or give him a chance to surrender, they just let fly.

Joanne screamed as Broderick slammed his body over hers, protecting her. Remy slid off the back of the horse, heading for cover.

Arrows plinked off the chainmail on Broderick's back. A few arrows stuck, penetrating the links to cut him beneath.

Then one of the Fae shot straight at the belly of the horse. The arrow went through it, and the dragon-horse died underneath Broderick.

It screamed and thrashed as it went down. Broderick grabbed Joanne and jumped clear of the horse with her, propelling her into the woods. Six more Fae rose in front of them with swords.

Broderick shoved Joanne out of their path and attacked them, his wolf claws coming out as he rose to the height of his between-beast.

The Fae were afraid of him, but they'd also just won a battle against other insanely violent Fae, and they dealt with the dragon-horses all the time. They had fear, but they fought through it.

The armor Broderick wore tore and split. His teeth and claws helped him fight, but in the end, his exhaustion and their overwhelming numbers brought him down. He fell, swords cutting him, a spear gouging him through the loosened chainmail into his back.

He saw Joanne held by Fae, and Remy as well. *At least we're together this time,* Broderick thought, right before a sword hilt smacked him in the skull.

KIAN INSISTED REMY AND JOANNE CONTINUE BUILDING their makeshift computer. They were taken to another tent, no longer confined to a solid-walled room, though guards were everywhere.

"Kian's not worried," Remy said. "He just saw that we

can't escape, that we have nowhere to go. They only have to grab us and pull us back."

"I'm so sorry you were caught in all this," Joanne said in a low voice to him. They were left relatively alone; even Daragh wasn't there.

Remy gave a mirthless laugh. "No, *you* were caught because of me. I was minding my own business, off on a mission thousands of miles from home, and *bam*, I was in this place. The Fae guy who captured me was thrilled to have someone from our world fall into his lap and decided to use me to help him invade. He forced me to start building a portal he could use anywhere … which I guess worked."

Joanne helped connect wires while she listened, but she knew she was hearing only half the tale. "It's not everyday someone finds themselves in a world they didn't know existed," she pointed out. "Didn't you freak? And how did they talk to you? I haven't understood a single word anyone's said to me."

"He knew a few words of English, enough to get his point across," Remy said. "I'd already been in a place unfamiliar to me—at first I thought I was just somewhere else in or around Afghanistan. Then I thought I'd been taken to Russia somewhere, then I finally figured out I wasn't in Kansas anymore. Then I focused on getting home. I've learned to compartmentalize."

Remy worked efficiently as he talked, quickly setting up what he had before. He'd explained to Daragh that he needed power to work it, but since they'd been left in here, no one had come.

"Your sister is happy," Joanne said. "She's with Seamus, now—he's a Feline Shifter."

One corner of Remy's mouth tilted up. "Yeah, Bree was always into Shifters."

"He's a great guy, and really cares for her. I think they'll be mated soon."

"Good for her." Remy's tone told Joanne he missed his sister with hard intensity, but he was bravely trying to hold it together. "What about the other Shifter with you? You two together?"

"Hell if I know." Joanne gave a short laugh. "We've been going out, and I'm in love with the lummox, but no, we're not mated or anything. I think he enjoys being a pain in my ass."

"He sure took a beating out there." Remy said. "He has a lot of courage."

Tears stung Joanne's eyes. The last she'd seen of Broderick, he'd been stuck full of arrows, with Fae beating on him. He'd been alive, roaring and cursing, fighting hard. Then Joanne had been pulled away, and she could get no confirmation that they hadn't killed him.

She found Remy's tanned, callused hand on hers. "Hey, we'll get out of this. And we'll find him. I don't leave anyone behind."

"Neither does he." Joanne blew out her breath. She needed to learn to compartmentalize, like Remy was doing, so she could focus. "What do we do now?"

Remy glanced at the boards they'd set up, the quartz ready to vibrate and produce signals. "We just need power, and then we can contact the other side."

Joanne remembered something Bree had told her. "*Was* it you haunting the attic? Your mom is convinced your ghost was up in the attic of her new house, which is on a ley line, Seamus says."

Remy stared at her. "I did try to figure out how to get

back across a couple times, tried to communicate, before I was caught. But I couldn't do it."

"Hmm. Well, maybe we can work that out once we open another gate and get home. Can you make sure no one is about to come in here?"

She spoke so casually that Remy didn't catch what she said for a moment. Then he, as casually, rose to his feet. "What do you have in mind?"

"I'll show you. Just make sure we have privacy."

Remy went to the slit in the tent that was the door to the room, lifted it with a finger and peered out. He stood motionlessly a moment, a well-built man in fatigues, his buzzed wheat-colored hair catching the lamplight. Again, Joanne had no idea what powered the lamps, but they weren't electric—they flickered with flame.

Remy strolled back to her. "Guards milling about, keeping an eye on us, but no Kian or Daragh heading this way."

"Good." Joanne slipped the medallion out of her pocket. When Broderick had slammed himself over her when the Fae were firing at them, he'd pressed the disc into her hand.

He knew he'd be captured, stripped, searched. He'd have nowhere to hide it. Joanne, they thought harmless. They'd shoved her and Remy back into the tents and ignored them.

Remy stared at the disc. "What the hell is that?" he asked, making sure his voice didn't carry.

"This is how we came over here in the first place," Joanne said. "I think so, anyway. Broderick had it, we had the code in place and a door frame, and it brought us through. I'm hoping it can take us back. It has magic in it, so I've been told."

Remy plucked it from her hand, examined the Celtic knot, and set it down carefully on the board. He let out a breath. "I've been here long enough to believe in anything. So why not?"

Joanne repositioned a few crystals to rest around the silver, and they waited.

I'M GETTING BLOODY SICK OF CAGES, BRODERICK THOUGHT, lying as wolf on the floor of another one. Its door was more secure than the previous, with a chain and a lock, and more wires to make his Collar go off if he touched them.

Broderick didn't know what they planned to do with him, but at least the head Fae hadn't killed him. Probably he wanted to use Broderick to fight for him, like Fae had since Shifters were born.

The thought percolated an idea through Broderick's brain, but he'd have to wait to act on it.

He'd given Joanne the medallion. She was smart enough to figure out a way to use it. She might be able to get herself to safety, and then she could round up Dylan and a few good Shifters like Spike and Ronan to come back and drag Broderick out of here.

Even if Dylan didn't want to rescue a good-for-nothing shithead like Broderick, Joanne would insist. So would Aunt Cora. It was nice to have two feisty females at his back.

Of course, if Broderick saw Tiger right now, he'd embrace him like a brother. The Fae wouldn't know what hit them if they had to face Tiger.

The idea in Broderick's tired mind began to solidify. He was a fighter—why not use that to his advantage?

Of course, he had to have energy and strength to make his plan work, and Broderick was fresh out of both. Being gouged by arrows, spears, and swords did that to a Shifter.

He lay in the cage, biding his time, thinking of Joanne. He though of every nuance of her—her warm lips, her body sliding beneath his in the dark, her smile that was only for him. Broderick had a treasure in her. She looked at *him* with a light in her eyes that was both tender and sexy.

Broderick pictured her lying on the floor with him, surrounded by the computers she loved, her hair against the black matting, her eyes half closed in pleasure. She knew him, understood him, welcomed him.

Mate.

Tiger, Goddess bless him, was right. Mating didn't have anything to do with the sun and moon ceremonies or the mate-claim, or fighting Challenges for her. Even the mating frenzy wasn't the whole story.

A mate was the other half of his whole. When both parts met, they sealed as one, didn't matter if a Shifter leader pronounced it, or Broderick said the right words. They were together, bound. The mate bond, the mystical part of the joining, didn't understand words or rituals. It just was.

The nugget of heat in Broderick's chest spread to his limbs, soothing him, helping his Shifter metabolism heal him. *The touch of a mate.*

Broderick gave a growling wolf laugh. *Even when the mate isn't with him.*

Kian, the Fae general of this bunch, and Daragh, the

deceased Guardian of the Montana Shiftertown, entered to interrupt Broderick's beautiful thoughts.

Broderick pulled himself to his feet, moving stiffly, the wolf snarling. Time to put the plan in motion and hope that Daragh, even though he was only a Feline, would be smart enough to catch on.

Broderick pushed himself up, no matter how much it hurt, and willed himself to shift to his between-beast. He could speak in this form, if raggedly.

"I'll kill you," he snarled, pointing at Daragh. "Enemy. Feline. You dragged me here." He slammed himself against the cage, putting up with the shocks that jerked through his Collar. "Enemy of my clan—I'll tear you apart."

CHAPTER SEVENTEEN

Kian looked interested at Broderick's declaration, as Broderick hoped he would. Though the Fae couldn't understand the words, he'd understand the tone of voice, the hatred in Broderick's eyes when he glared at Daragh.

Daragh blinked a few times, then his body stiffened as he caught on to what Broderick was doing. Well, Felines were slow.

He translated what Broderick had said, then Daragh sent a ferocious and very Feline snarl back at Broderick. "Stupid-ass fighter," he said. "That's all you Lupines can do. Meet me in the ring—and we'll see."

"Tough words from a man *outside* the cage," Broderick said. "Tell him—tell him what a bastard you are and that I want a chance to rip you into tiny Feline pieces. I don't care if you're dead already—I can still hurt you."

Daragh rapidly spoke to Kian, who continued to look interested. Kian sent a flood of words back to Daragh.

Daragh kept the hostile look on his face while he translated to Broderick. "He says he wants to watch us

fight. In a ring we can't escape from—a Fae-style challenge. He says his men need something to entertain them
after their victory." Daragh snarled, and added for the
benefit of any who might understand them. "Be prepared
to die, Lupine."

Broderick only growled back, sliding down into his
pure wolf form. *Good answer, Feline. You might actually be
intelligent.*

Broderick had bought a way out of his cage. Now to
find out if he could escape what the Fae thought of as an
entertaining fight, grab Joanne, and haul ass out of here.
That Joanne was busy doing her part to free them, Broderick had no doubt.

He could count on his mate.

A SPARK CRACKLED AROUND THE QUARTZ AND
makeshift tubes. Joanne jumped, having dozed off.
They'd sat for hours waiting for something to happen,
and Joanne, exhausted, couldn't keep her eyes open.

Remy, as alert and fresh as ever, stared with clear blue
eyes at the medallion.

"Damn," he whispered. "That can't work."

"It's magic—just go with it," Joanne murmured back,
trying to keep the excitement out of her voice. No need to
alert the guards.

Remy picked up two wires, stripped the ends, and
started tapping them together. "This is sort of what I did
before. I lost half my equipment when this bunch of Fae
slaughtered the other bunch of Fae. *That* was fun." His
bleak look told her it had been anything but.

"This has to do *something*," Joanne said, sitting so that

her body hid his from any guard who might peek into the room. "Code, Sergeant. Code like the wind."

Remy tapped rapidly, sending signals Joanne couldn't identify. What they were wasn't the point. The point would be having them reach someone who could help them.

She heard commotion outside the tent and moved to look out. Five Fae guards stood solidly at the entrance, but beyond them, in the corridors of the pavilion, soldiers were talking, laughing excitedly, giving each other a hard time, in the way of males everywhere.

Joanne kept watch, ready to alert Remy if anyone headed for them. Remy kept on making sparks, sending pulses to who knew where.

He'd just set down the wires with a sigh, rubbing his arms, when the medallion rang on its own.

Joanne hurriedly crossed the room, hovering over the board. The medallion's music faded, then it started again, but in exact bursts.

"Is it her?" she whispered excitedly. "Cilla?"

"I don't know," Remy answered, as excited as she was. "At this point, I don't care."

"Tell them to be ready," Joanne said. "Tell them to put together the door frame. We need to figure out a way to get Broderick."

Remy started in, but a few seconds later, Joanne heard voices coming toward them, and then guards snapped back the canvas.

Remy dropped the wires and yanked them from the sockets at the same time Joanne snatched up the medallion and shoved it back into the pocket of her jeans.

The guards pointed swords and knives at them and motioned them to follow. As soon as Joanne came to them, one caught her arm and dragged her along, the point of a dagger pricking through her shirt to her side.

Remy was pulled behind. He didn't fight, and neither did Joanne. Better to find out where they were being taken first.

Instead of entering another tent in this sea of tents, they were propelled into the woods. Joanne's heart beat faster. Were they being taken out to be killed?

After about five minutes of walking, they emerged into another clearing, this one packed with Fae. The Fae made a circle around a large open area, and the energy was electric. The Fae soldiers were avid, eager, drunk with their triumph over their enemies and whatever liquid they passed around.

On one side of the circle was a cage, in the cage, Broderick. He was in wolf form, glaring out with his white-gray eyes, ears back, snarling.

On the other side of the circle, Daragh.

Daragh had stripped out of his clothes, and now stood naked and upright, his Collar gleaming. He faced Broderick across the bare space and growled back at him.

"What the hell?" Joanne cried.

Daragh heard her and glanced over. "Battle. He challenged me. I had to answer."

Joanne's mouth hung open. She wanted to ask more questions, such as *why?* but something in Daragh's eyes made her fall silent.

Another Fae, this one with red beads braided through his long white-blond hair, stepped into the middle of the ring. He shouted something, pointing to Broderick. When he paused, the soldiers cheered, raising fists, the noise surging to a wildness.

The red-beaded Fae shouted again, this time pointing

at Daragh. Again, the Fae screamed and yelled. Daragh was the favorite, Broderick the challenger.

"Doesn't seem fair," Remy said in Joanne's ear. "Broderick has to fight a man who's already dead. Kind of gives Daragh an advantage."

"Yeah, I think the Fae are loving that," she said back.

The Fae in the middle held up his arms, while the soldiers went crazy. Amid the noise, the announcer stepped back out of the way—rapidly—and another Fae flung open the door of Broderick's cage.

Broderick charged out. Daragh ran at him, shifting halfway across the makeshift arena, and the two—wolf and leopard—clashed together in a ball of claws and fur.

The Fae around them screamed, shouted. Kian was on Broderick's side of the ring, looking on from among his men. He had a satisfied smile on his face.

As the noise from the Fae soldiers rose, Joanne was distracted by a jangling hum, a hot vibration in the area of her left hip. The medallion.

She thrust her hand into her pocket and closed her fingers around it. It burned her, but Joanne held on tight.

In a few seconds, she couldn't hear the Fae and the snarling in the middle of the ring as the Shifters fought. The tinkling of music came to her, and the thrum of vibrating strings, which rose around her until they blotted out all else.

———

BRODERICK FOUGHT AND BIT, TUMBLED DOWN INTO the dirt with a couple hundred pounds of fighting leopard on top of him. Daragh was going to make this as real as possible.

Of course, the Fae would want to see the two Shifters
fight. They loved watching what they thought of as lesser
beings battle to the death.

Well, they'd get a show. Broderick shifted to his
between-beast and so did Daragh. They faced each other,
arms spread, a huge wolf creature and an equally large
leopard creature ready to fight. Daragh's green eyes were
alight, touched with gold, and Daragh smiled.

"Bring it, Lupine."

He was enjoying himself, the shit. Daragh must have
been something in his fight club. Being a prisoner here
had denied him that—had taken him from his family, his
friends, everything he loved and cared about. Broderick
determined to change that.

At least he would if Daragh let Broderick live through
the fight. The soldiers wound up with noise as Daragh
charged Broderick. The two Shifters met, grunting,
sweating, grappling.

Broderick's Collar went off, biting pain into him. A
second later, so did Daragh's. Kian watched, eyes gleaming, waiting for the Shifters to go down in a wash
of agony.

Broderick bared his teeth at Kian. "Suck on it!" he
yelled, then he was fighting hard with Daragh again.

In this form the two Shifters could use fists as well as
teeth and claws. Daragh got Broderick in a lock, raking
big cat claws down his side. Broderick's fur turned most
of it, but blood flowed.

The Fae loved the blood. They couldn't get enough of
it, judging from the noise they made. Broderick clawed a
hole in Daragh's side, but nothing came out—he was
fighting a corpse.

"Don't think you have an edge because you're dead,"

Broderick snarled. "Shit, I can only say something like that in this fucking place."

Daragh didn't wait for him to finish. He attacked Broderick, and they met again, fighting, tearing, biting, while the Fae went crazy around them.

Out of the corner of his eye, when the fight took him in the right direction, Broderick saw Joanne. She was standing slightly behind the blond soldier, he in a protective stance in front of her. Whatever the hell she was doing, Broderick couldn't tell. She had the medallion, and she was smart. Joanne would think of something.

Daragh spun Broderick in a circle. Broderick locked hands around the man's furry neck and spun him back.

As he did, Broderick saw Joanne's outline distinctly waver. He focused on the fight, pretending he didn't notice.

Remy sidled to his right, effectively blocking Kian's view of Joanne, but Broderick saw her. Her entire body flickered, as though Broderick were seeing a weak projection of a movie. Then, Joanne winked out. Gone.

Broderick roared. Every Fae head, including Kian's, turned his way. When Broderick chanced another glance, Remy too had vanished.

They were gone. A scan of the Fae showed they were no longer in the crowd, or in the clearing. They'd been at the front, where Kian could keep an eye on them. Any second now, Kian would look over and realize they were gone.

Broderick roared again, drawing himself up, letting Daragh tackle him. The Fae yelled for their favorite, surging forward. Broderick fought back, hard, for his life. Daragh couldn't afford to give him any quarter.

It was worth it, a dim corner of Broderick's mind

reflected as the rest of his body focused on the fight. His challenge had created the diversion Joanne needed to get away. Even if Broderick died here, he wouldn't regret what he'd done. Joanne would be home, safe from these bloodthirsty bastards. She'd go on with her life, her work, would be there for her sister, would live and love, as it should be.

Of course, if Broderick could get out of here alive, so much the better.

He wasn't sure how he was going to manage it. Unless he could run away from this camp, find his way through a world he knew nothing about, stumble upon a ley line and figure out how it worked to let him through, he was pretty much stuck here.

As he got Daragh into another lock, Daragh biting the hell out of Broderick's arm, Kian turned his head, looked to where Joanne and Remy should be standing, and saw that they were missing.

Kian came alert, searching the crowd for them. His amusement at the fight died and rage took its place.

Kian strode to the guards who were supposed to have been watching the two, took out his knife, and held it up to them, yelling something. The guards looked suddenly terrified—likely they'd pay for their lapse with their lives.

Kian was shouting, striding through the ranks. Broderick and Daragh fought on, the Fae still calling for blood. Kian broke through to the center of the ring, raised his knife high, commanding all attention. He then lowered the knife to point straight at Broderick, fury in every line of him.

He shouted one word. Broderick didn't understand it, but from the blood-lust filled eyes that turned on him from every single Fae, he didn't need a translation.

Kill.

Daragh, who'd been trying to rake his claws across Broderick's abdomen the second before, released him and stood shoulder to shoulder with him, facing the onslaught.

"Hey, you tried," Daragh said to him.

"My mate is free," Broderick answered with conviction. "That's all that matters."

"One thing." Daragh snarled as he faced the onslaught of armed Fae. "If we'd been in a fight club at home, I'd have kicked your ass."

"That fight wasn't over, cat-breath," Broderick managed, and then the Fae were upon them.

CHAPTER EIGHTEEN

J oanne found herself falling to a cement floor,
surrounded by the music of the boxes, the hum of
computers, the bright light of day coming in
through the high windows, and Shifters.

Mason pulled her upright, the look in his eyes one of
terrible worry. "Broderick?"

"Still in there. Hang on."

Joanne swung around, shivering, gripping the medallion. Behind her was the doorframe, two upright wooden
posts and a lintel, held in place by Spike and Seamus.
Tiger stood beyond, his eyes a hot yellow. Cilla sat in
front of the computers, breathing hard, terrified.

Joanne reached back through the opening. Instantly,
she felt the cold of the Fae night, heard the roar of Fae
urging on the fighters, smelled the blood, the rank dampness of the woods.

She also saw the broad fatigue-covered shoulders of
Remy Fayette. Joanne grabbed him and dragged him
to her.

Remy jumped through and nearly fell on top of Joanne.

Instantly, the sounds of the fight faded, and the warmth of an Austin spring morning returned. Joanne spun around once with Remy, as though they danced, Remy's blue gaze taking everything in.

He recognized computers, power tools, fluorescent lights, old brick walls, and the very human Cilla, everything to tell him he was back in the ordinary human world, in an ordinary warehouse, the sounds of a city coming in through the windows.

Remy let out a strangled cry of delight and relief, then he fell facedown on the floor. "Thank God," he said fervently. He kissed the cement floor with an audible smack. "Thank God!"

Seamus looked down at him. "Goddess, are they all like that?"

"Seamus, this is Remy," Joanne said breathlessly. "Bree's brother. He was trapped in Faerie—will tell you all about it later. Right now, we need to get Broderick. Tiger, help move this doorframe. Over there a little. There's about a thousand angry, armed Fae between us and him."

Seamus gave Remy a shocked look then he helped Spike and Tiger reposition the doorway. Joanne said a prayer, hoped to hell she was right, clutched the medallion, and dove back through.

BRODERICK WAS GOING TO DIE. HE KNEW IT. IT WAS A matter of time before a Fae sword went right through some vital part of him.

Daragh protected Broderick the best he could. Knives went into him, the Fae beat on him, but Daragh couldn't be killed. He'd take it as long as he was able, though Daragh's Collar was going off and he was in terrible pain.

Broderick was in pain as well, and his Collar was buzzing like crazy, but damned if he'd let these Fae know how much he hurt.

In the midst of all this he heard ... music. Familiar music. Son of a bitch.

Joanne walked out of thin air into a melee of Fae. Broderick shouted, tried to get to her, but there were too many on him.

Joanne disappeared instantly, then a few seconds later, she materialized again, only closer. Broderick roared and threw off his attackers, trying to reach her.

He saw her take a step, and another, then Kian, the bastard, reached out and seized her.

Broderick had the soldiers off him before he knew he'd done it. He threw bodies aside, his berserker rage filling his blood.

He was a few feet away. Kian had a firm hold of Joanne, and his knife was coming up to her throat.

"Get your fucking hands off my *mate!*" Broderick yelled as he flung himself at them.

The words got tangled in his mouth, and all that came out was *My! Mate!*

Broderick reached Kian, grabbed him. At least twenty Fae at Broderick's back seized him, ready to kill. Joanne screamed and struggled. She latched her hand around Broderick's arm, tugging him.

Broderick felt the thrum of the medallion through her touch. He clamped his hand around hers, hanging on.

The Fae didn't want that. They rose up around Broderick and Joanne cutting off their retreat.

Broderick fought, but he knew they were done. They were going to die here in Faerie, fuck it all …

… and then two things happened that changed everything.

Daragh surged up in the middle of the Fae like the wrath of the Goddess. He'd gotten hold of a sword, and he slashed the soldiers out of Broderick's way.

He'd wielded a sword since his Choosing, and though the Sword of the Guardian was a magical blade that released souls, it was also a damn good weapon. Daragh proved he knew swordsmanship, turning aside blades and fighting around to engage Kian one on one.

The second thing that saved them came through the doorframe a few seconds later, a giant of a Shifter, half changed into a very pissed off, bigger than hell Bengal tiger.

Tiger grabbed the Fae in his way, threw them aside like so much used tissue, and clamped one big hand each on Broderick and Joanne.

"Go!" Daragh shouted behind them. "And do it, Lupine. Promise me."

Broderick met his gaze, the Feline one holding desperation, but over that, grim determination to go down swinging.

"You got it, big guy," Broderick said. "Goddess go with you."

He barely got out the words. Kian, with skill that matched Daragh's, slashed into Daragh's gut, then he pressed his sword into Daragh's Collar. Daragh screamed in agony, falling to his knees.

Broderick saw the other Fae go at Daragh to cut him

to pieces, right before Tiger threw them both through the door.

Broderick landed on cold cement, surrounded by his brother, Spike and Seamus, and then Tiger. Broderick kicked at the doorframe and it fell apart. The hum of the medallion died, and the music boxes stopped.

Broderick simply lay on the hard floor and breathed, blood flowing out of him, every limb aching.

But he had Joanne. He rolled over onto his back, and Joanne dropped to her knees beside him, taking his face between her hands, kissing him repeatedly.

Broderick's mating frenzy rose, fed by the fight, his fear and anger, his need. Joanne was all right. Broderick hadn't lost her.

Broderick closed his arms around her and pulled her down to him, pinning her against him. "Joanne Greene," he said, the words hoarse in his raw throat. "By the Goddess and in front of witnesses, I claim you as mate!"

The last phrase rang high against the ceiling. Mason said, "Holy shit," and Spike chuckled. "About time, dick brain."

Joanne ignored them. She smiled into Broderick's eyes, her own full of love and relief. "Okay," she said.

The mate frenzy kicked in hard. Broderick rolled over again, putting Joanne under him, taking her mouth. He needed her, now, now—screw those around them. They could leave or deserve what they saw.

It hurt—it nearly killed him, to rein in his hunger. Broderick raised his head and gazed at Joanne, her beautiful face, and the knowledge in her eyes. She understood.

"I made a promise," Broderick said, and Joanne nodded, a sadness entering her expression. Daragh deserved to rest.

Broderick pointed a stern finger at Cilla, who watched them, wide-eyed. "Now, *you* tell me where the fucking Sword of the Guardian is, so I can keep my word."

CILLA HAD STASHED THE SWORD UNDER THE floorboards in an old trailer house on the northern outskirts of San Antonio. Sean accompanied them on the trip, which made Cilla nervous, but Joanne only had so much sympathy for her.

Tiger, Sean, Broderick, and Joanne squeezed into the trailer with her, waiting while Cilla pried up the floor and removed the sword, which she'd wrapped in a blanket.

Sean took the sword and unwrapped it, briefly closed his eyes, and whispered a prayer over it. Then he reached out to Broderick, expecting Broderick to give him the medallion that fit on the end of the hilt.

Broderick studied the medallion on his palm. "I can't."

Sean's brows went up. He looked Broderick up and down. Tiger, who usually was an enforcer for the Morrisseys, stepped to Broderick, supporting him.

Sean let out his breath, turned the sword blade-down, and handed it to Broderick. "I guess it's up to you," he said.

Broderick held the sword in his left hand, and with his right, cupped the medallion against the end of the hilt.

Joanne heard a hiss, then a hum. When Broderick lifted his hand away, the silver of the disc had fused with that of the sword, making it a whole piece, without a seam.

Broderick lowered his arm, but Joanne saw him

wince. Joanne grabbed his wrist and turned his hand over again. In the center of his palm, etched as though burned there, was the symbol of the Celtic knot. The medallion had branded him.

"Can you get out of here now?" Cilla asked, voice sullen. "I have things to do."

"Nope." Joanne latched her hand around the girl's wrist. "You are coming to Montana with us and seeing this through."

Cilla's dark eyes filled with tears. "I never meant for the Guardian to be killed. I didn't tell them to."

"You can explain to his family," Joanne said firmly. "They deserve that."

Sean said, "We've already rounded up the men you hired. Dad had a word with them."

Sean left it hanging, but Cilla paled. Joanne didn't know Dylan well, but she had come to learn that when Dylan "had a word" with someone, that word tended to be permanent. Those who incurred Dylan's wrath often were never heard from again.

On their way to the airstrip where they'd meet the cargo plane to take them north, Joanne directed Sean to stop at Bree's mom's house. They'd left Remy there on their way to San Antonio, but he'd expressed a wish to go with them, to pay his respects to Daragh, who'd sacrificed so much.

When they arrived, it was to find Bree and her mother on either side of Remy on the couch, the two women clinging to him. Seamus was there, leaning on the newel post of the stairway, watching them fondly, but giving the family room to connect.

"Decided not to go with you," Remy said when Seamus let them in. He looked happy with his arms around his sister and mom, all of them with red-rimmed eyes. "We need to be together for a while."

Seamus's eyes were wet as well—he was an empath, and the emotions of Bree and her family caught him too, rolling him over in feeling. He shared their joy as no one else could.

Bree untangled herself from the trio and came to Joanne. Bree's hair was the same honey color as Remy's, her eyes as blue.

Bree pulled Joanne into a hug. "Thank you for bringing him home."

"My pleasure," Joanne said. "I bet he has a long and bizarre story to tell you."

"If he can talk while my mom stuffs him full of food," Bree said, grinning. "That's her way of telling us she loves us. Plus, she hasn't lit a cigarette since Seamus brought him in the door."

Joanne hugged Bree again, waved at Remy, who would be planted on that sofa for some time, she saw, and departed. Time to pay one last visit.

THE RIDE IN THE BACK OF THE CARGO PLANE TO Montana gave Broderick time to have his arms around Joanne and simply breathe.

Her hair smelled like roses, since she'd showered before they left, with the bath products she liked to use. Mason complained that their bathroom smelled like a lady's salon, but Mason would understand when he started looking for a mate. Plus, Broderick told Mason, Joanne smelled a hell of a lot better than his three sweaty brothers.

The plane bumped along, the makeshift seats uncomfortable, but Broderick didn't mind. He had Joanne on his lap, snuggled against him. Everything was good.

Daragh's Sword of the Guardian lay in a sheath next to Broderick. Sean had offered to carry it, but Broderick insisted. He didn't want to let it go, not yet. His reluctance bugged him, and he didn't like what it might imply. But for now, Broderick had to do what he had to do.

Cilla huddled in a seat by herself, under the watchful eyes of Spike and Tiger. She looked miserable, but Broderick understood why Joanne insisted she come with them.

The girl needed to learn that every action, large or small, had consequences. Just because Cilla couldn't see the people she was hurting, didn't mean they weren't hurt, and didn't deserve some reparation. The fact that Cilla had helped drag Remy and Joanne out of Faerie, plus had been coerced by one of the scumbag Fae, gave her some points with Broderick. Though weighed against Daragh's death, the balance was still not in her favor.

Broderick at first had wondered whether Cilla and her crew, or the Fae, had been behind blowing up the munitions plant as well, but Dylan said no, according to Sean. Dylan seemed to know all about it, but he wouldn't say anything more.

The leader of the Shiftertown in Montana, Eoin Lyall, met them at the plane and drove them into Shiftertown himself. It was deep in the woods, cities few and far between in this area. Ranchers and farmers didn't want Shifters nearby, so they lived in a place that was remote, dimly lit because of the thick canopy of trees, and a bit wild.

The large house Daragh and his family occupied lay

in the center of this Shiftertown. Shifters came out to watch Eoin drive Broderick, Joanne, and Sean through the twisting roads to the heart of their community. Spike and Tiger came behind with Cilla, driven by Eoin's second.

Daragh had been laid out in the living room of the house, on a plain, single bed that was likely his own. He lay in state, with candles burning around him, in this public room so that other Shifters could come to pay their respects and say prayers over him. They'd dressed him in the clothes similar to the ones Broderick had seen him in, jeans and T-shirt, as though they wanted him to be as comfortable as possible.

As soon as they were admitted, Joanne slipped her hand from Broderick's and went to Daragh's still body, laying her hand on his shoulder. "I hate seeing him like this."

Broderick joined her, looking down at the Shifter who'd sacrificed himself to save their lives. "I'm thinking he's not too thrilled with it either."

Joanne glanced up at Daragh's family—his mother, his brother, and a sister. Daragh hadn't been mated, had no cubs. Broderick burned inside. Daragh should have had the chance to find a mate, fall in love, be a dad.

"He was a good man," Joanne told them. "Fearless."

His mother, a dignified Feline Shifter, gave Joanne a nod. "We know. Thank you, child."

Tiger came forward, his fingers on Cilla's shoulder. He didn't drag her, but Broderick knew Cilla had no choice but to go where Tiger wanted her to.

Daragh's family obviously knew who Cilla was. Sean would have filled them in when he told them Broderick and party were coming. The brother and sister had deep anger in their eyes, but Daragh's mother simply looked at Cilla.

"I'm sorry," Cilla said, tears in her voice. "I'm so sorry."

Daragh's mother reached over from where she sat and took Cilla's hand. "I've had a chance to think since Daragh was killed," she said. "You can waste a lot of time on guilt and grief. You were caught in ambition and greed, which can enslave any one of us. You were forced into aiding the Fae but then decided to help another caught in his power. Daragh died for that, gave his life so a man could be saved. That is the memory I will keep."

Cilla sat down next to her and cried. Daragh's mother put a soothing arm around her, but she watched Broderick and Joanne.

Broderick rumbled, "He gave his life several times over. I'm going bring him a little peace."

Without waiting for anything else—no speeches, prayers, or rituals—Broderick unsheathed Daragh's sword.

The blade rang softly, the runes dancing in the candle-light. The candle flames around Daragh rose higher as Broderick passed the sword above them.

Broderick placed his hand over Daragh's heart. "Rest easy my friend. And yeah, maybe you would have kicked my ass. We can have a rematch in the Summerland."

He curled his fingers on Daragh's chest, then withdrew his hand. Flipping the sword over, Broderick rested it point down over Daragh's heart. He drew a breath, and thrust it home.

The candle flames shot high then dropped back down to the merest flicker. Broderick swore he saw Daragh's body stiffen, then it shimmered, became nothing but dust motes that glittered in the candlelight, then collapsed down onto the empty bed.

Broderick heard a sigh, felt a breath of wind touch his face, faint laughter on the breeze. The laughter held relief and not an ounce of pain.

Thank you, a whisper sounded, and then faded to silence.

CHAPTER NINETEEN

S tay." Eoin Lyall stopped Broderick outside Daragh's
house as the Austin Shifters headed back to the
vehicles.

Joanne slipped her hand into Broderick's, feeling the
warmth around the burn the medallion had left. Her heart
had lightened once she'd seen Daragh become dust — his
soul freed. She wished she could have seen the expres-
sions on the faces of the Fae when he disappeared from
their clutches.

"Stay, why?" Broderick asked Eoin. "I have things to
do at home, a mating to schedule, brothers to yell at."

"We'll have another Choosing." Eoin pinned Broderick
with his Feline stare. "We have no Guardian. *You* sent
Daragh to the Goddess, not Sean. She might choose you."

The look in Eoin's eyes told Joanne he believed with
all his heart that the Goddess would touch Broderick,
that She'd simply been waiting for him to appear.

"No," Broderick said sharply. He held Daragh's
sword, which he still carried, up by its hilt. "Not only no,

but hell no. Double hell no. I'm not going to be a fucking Guardian."

Sean, who'd stopped next to him, blinked, but offered no criticism.

"Here." Broderick pushed the sword at Eoin. "Take it. I don't ever want to see it again."

Eoin hesitated. Broderick let go of the hilt, and Eoin caught the sword before it fell.

Broderick had no trouble giving the sword back, Joanne noticed. When he'd had the medallion, and when they'd retrieved the sword from Cilla, he'd been very protective, not wanting anyone else to touch sword or medallion unless he let them. That compulsion seemed to be over.

"Let's go," Broderick said to Spike and Tiger. "We have a plane to catch."

"Wait a sec." Joanne looked back to the porch, where Cilla stood next to Daragh's mother. His mother already looked more relieved, her worry about Daragh's soul gone, though her grief would doubtless never leave her. "Cilla, are you coming?"

Cilla shook her head. "I'm going to stay here. I'll try to help them — for whatever that's worth."

Daragh's mother nodded. "We'll look after her."

And they would, Joanne understood, with an intensity only Shifters could manage. Cilla needed that, Joanne realized, a discipline her life had lacked.

Joanne nodded at Cilla, acknowledging her self-imposed penance. Sean had told them that Dylan, with the help of Fionn, had been searching for the Fae who'd hurt Cilla's former boyfriend, but so far they'd found nothing. Either the Fae had gone back to Faerie or was hiding very well. Now that his master was dead, he likely would stay hidden.

"All right," Joanne said to Cilla. "But the next time you get in over your hacker head *call me.*" Joanne mimicked holding a phone to her ear and gave Cilla a stern look.

"I will," Cilla said. "Promise."

Once the plane was rumbling under them, heading home, Joanne laid her head on Broderick's shoulder.

"I guess the sword chose you," she said.

"What?" Broderick roused himself from a half sleep. The plane's drone was soothing, all the Shifters drooping. Spike was stretched out on a hard bench, one tattooed arm over his eyes.

"I said, the sword chose you." Joanne repeated.

Broderick's gray eyes flickered. "What the hell is that supposed to mean?"

"*You* found the medallion, which fell off the sword, no one else. You didn't want to let it go. You got into Faerie and found Daragh, and then you sent him to dust. Not Sean, not Tiger, not Spike. You."

"You're the one who got us into Faerie," Broderick reminded her, "whether we liked it or not. I just stumbled in."

"Because you had the medallion, which also let me into the Guardian Network so I could learn how to program the portal. It wanted us to find Daragh and release him."

Broderick's arms tightened around her. "Huh. If it wanted us to save him, why not simply lead us to the sword so we could go to Montana right away? Why waste time with Faerie?"

"So you could meet Daragh and *want* to help him,

instead of just sending Sean up there to do it. Plus, we had to find and free Remy." Joanne tapped Broderick's chest. "Face it, big guy, you were the Chosen One."

"God and Goddess spare me," Broderick growled. "Next time, someone else can be chosen. And I'm not going to be a Guardian. No way, no how. The Goddess can suck it up."

"Not you." Tiger, who'd been asleep, or so it seemed, opened his eyes and bathed Broderick in a yellow stare. He flicked the gaze to Joanne, then back to Broderick. "Your cub."

Broderick stopped. So did Joanne. "Wait, wait, wait a second," Broderick said. "What are you talking about?"

"Joanne is carrying your cub. Take that cub to a Choosing, and he will be Guardian."

Joanne stared at him in shock. "Cub? No, we just ..." She broke off, face heating.

"From that mating will come a cub," Tiger said, unembarrassed. "He will one day bear a Guardian's sword."

Spike was awake now, listening avidly. Sean burst into musical laughter. "You're for it now, Brod," Sean said. "Tiger's never wrong about these things."

Joanne placed her hand on her abdomen and leaned against Broderick, her heart beating rapidly. A cub. With Broderick. Terrifying ... and so, so wonderful.

Broderick stared, openmouthed. "Tiger, you are one seriously scary Shifter, you know that?"

Tiger looked annoyed a moment, then his expression cleared. "Not scary to Carly. Or to my cub. Come and see him when he's born." His brows drew together again. "But not too close."

Joanne pealed with laughter at that. Sean joined her,

Spike gave his silent smile, and only Broderick went on growling.

But that was Broderick, and what he did. Joanne would take him and his snarling growls over all the laughter in the world.

"WHY DID YOU BRING ME BACK HERE?" JOANNE ASKED Broderick a day later.

They stood in his warehouse, truly alone this time, because Broderick had threatened his brothers with dire fates if they went anywhere near it this afternoon. And evening. Maybe all night.

Broderick liked the way Joanne looked admiringly over all he'd created, marveling at the workmanship, intricacy, artistry.

But now she was done with the tour and wanted answers.

"Why do you think I brought you here?" he asked her.

"Privacy," Joanne said. She gave Broderick a little smile. Well, she wasn't naive. "But we could have had privacy at my house."

"There's more here," Broderick said. "No neighbors to call the police if it gets too loud."

Joanne's smile widened. "Will it get loud?"

Broderick gave up being subtle and stepped against her. "I'm barely holding it in, Jo-Jo. I've been in mating frenzy for you for days, but I've been busy fighting for my life and saving people and doing whatever a stupid-ass piece of metal wanted me to. But now that's over, and I get to do what *I* want to."

He seized Joanne around the waist and lifted her to a high workbench, which he'd made sure he'd cleaned off before he brought her here.

Joanne rested her arms on his shoulders. "Yeah? And what exactly do you want to do?"

"Have you ever seen a Shifter in mating frenzy?"

"No." Joanne rubbed the back of his neck.

"It's not pretty. It's not champagne and roses. It's raw, and real. What we did before was tame."

Joanne leaned forward and pressed a kiss to the tip of his nose. "You're my mate. So you keep saying. I assume mating frenzy leaves both mates intact?"

Broderick could barely nod. The frenzy was gripping him, dissolving anything civilized.

Joanne wrapped her arms tighter around him. "Then stop worrying about it," she said.

The next moment, she squealed as Broderick tore her shirt straight off. She wore a thin silky shirt with spaghetti straps underneath instead of a bra, and Broderick tore that off too.

She rocked back in a denim skirt and bare chest, her startled cries turning to laughter.

Broderick had her planted farther back on the workbench before he ripped off her skirt and panties, then paused to claw off his own clothes.

He parted her legs and stepped between them, pulling her close and growling.

Mate. My mate!

The first plunge into her was sweet. Joanne spread her legs wider, urging him in. Broderick lowered her back onto the high workbench while he stood, thrusting into her. He loved how her head rocked, her body arched, how she clung to his wrists with fingers that left marks.

The sex was basic and primal. Beautiful. Joanne shrieked and yelled, laughed and screamed. Broderick wasn't silent—he shouted, groaned, let himself plunge into every brilliant second of it.

"I love you!" Joanne said, her words ringing through the room.

"Love you, Jo-Jo. Love you so much. You beautiful, beautiful woman."

Broderick held her thighs, fingers tight, as he thrust hard. Joanne's words grew incoherent, as jumbled as his thoughts.

Mate, love, fucking sweet, want to be in you forever …

Without a conscious decision to do so, Broderick lifted his hand, the one imprinted with the Celtic knot, and laid it between Joanne's breasts, over her heart.

A hot sensation jumped from there to his own heart, and Joanne sucked in a sharp breath, looking stunned.

The mate bond. He knew it. Tiger had known it.

The joy that had eluded Broderick all his life, the one he'd pursued without understanding, folded itself around him. His Joanne carried his cub, and Broderick was complete.

Didn't mean he was going to abandon the mating frenzy and weep with happiness. Broderick kept thrusting into her, the erotic sensations twining with love and making everything three times as hot.

They both ended up on the workbench, Joanne's legs wrapped around Broderick's torso as he joined with the woman he loved.

When they came, it was intense. Broderick could barely breathe, had lost all power of speech, and only groaned when his seed left him to bury itself inside

Joanne. Joanne laughed and cried out, wrapped herself even tighter around him, and held on as they rode it out.

After a long time, they wound down, holding each other, kissing lightly, then more strongly with hot, loving kisses. The mate bond heated the air between them.

Broderick's palm tingled, and then the music boxes began to play. Not with the jangle that had announced the opening of the gate to Faerie, but with a soft, muted tone that sweetened the air.

To the music of what Broderick and his family had created, he and Joanne held each other, touching, kissing. It was the beginning of a long time of happiness to come, but the happiness of the moment was overwhelming.

Joanne kissed him, her smile warm. The silvery music wound with the mate bond and sealed two halves into a whole.

End

Mason McNaughton jolted out of a sound sleep as several hundred pounds of enraged Feline landed on his chest and started to rip the hell out of him.

Mason rolled out from under the deadly claws, shifting as he went. He came up in his half-wolf form, grabbed the Feline around the waist and threw him into the wall. The wildcat bounced off and used the momentum to crash back into Mason.

They both went down, landing on the edge of the bed, which collapsed. The wooden frame splintered, the mattress sliding off and pinning Mason with the Feline on top of him. Mason's Collar triggered, shocking and sparking pain into his own neck, but if he stopped fighting, he'd die.

Mason's half-beast form gave him the strength to battle for his life. It also let him yell.

"Son of a bitch, get this fucking feral off me!"

He already heard running in the hallway and his oldest brother, Broderick, burst into the room with his usual energy. Broderick grabbed the snarling, spitting Feline and tried to yank him away from Mason.

The Feline turned around and went for Broderick, who was still in human form and wearing nothing but a small pair of boxer briefs. Broderick's skin reddened with blood as the Feline's claws raked his unprotected skin.

Mason launched himself off the floor, landing on the Feline and dragging him from Broderick. Broderick was swearing and bleeding but came back fighting.

"Aleck!" Broderick shouted at the Feline. *"Stop!"*

The Feline didn't even acknowledge his own name. He was far gone in the feral state, snarling and biting, his green cat eyes a crazed and burning red.

They'd have to kill the bastard this time for sure. What if he hadn't burst into Mason's room but Broderick and Joanna's, or Aunt Cora's?

Mason wrestled the Feline down, his wolf claws raking through the cat's fur, drawing blood. Broderick was shifting, Mason saw out of the corner of his eye. The feral Aleck was a writhing ball of wildness, ready to slaughter everyone in the room, the house, maybe all of Shiftertown.

Mason knew they wouldn't be able to stop him short of breaking his neck. Aleck's mate was about ready to drop a cub, and killing him would bring her terrible grief. But they had to stop him before he slaughtered the rest of the house.

Broderick became his full gray wolf and landed in the fray. He and Mason dodged giant cat paws and the snarling mouth, the wildcat's ears flat on his head. Aleck had no idea who they were—who *he* was. He was only killing the Lupines, threats to his mate, no matter that Aleck was alive at all because of Mason and his brothers.

Aleck, unlike Broderick and Mason, didn't wear a shock Collar. Broderick's Collar was sparking as deeply as Mason's, slowing him down, while Aleck was free to surrender to the deadly violence that lurked inside every Shifter.

They couldn't delay any longer. Mason saw that thought flash through Broderick's eyes as well. Mason moved to grab the Feline in a headlock. He would break Aleck's neck and take the fall for it — Broderick couldn't do it, because he was alpha and would need to calm down the rest of the family when Aleck was dead. Mason was expendable, at the bottom of this family's little pack.

The Feline slipped out of Mason's hold, turned around, and sank every one of his front claws into Mason's stomach, tearing it open. Mason's yell mixed with a howl as his full wolf took over. His reason faded as the crazed battle beast rose up inside him, and he went for the kill.

He barely heard the noise just inside the doorway, but a second later, Broderick was tumbling Mason out of the way. There was a soft bang, a thunk, and the Feline let out a cat shriek that drilled into Mason's brain and stayed there.

The Feline's scream died to a whimper. He collapsed in a tangle of limbs and tail, his green eyes half closing as his breathing wound down into that of peaceful sleep.

Mason dragged his head up. In the doorway stood Joanne, Broderick's mate, her hair sleep tousled, her nightshirt dragging down one shoulder. She peered over the barrel of a tranq rifle, eyeing Aleck to make sure he stayed asleep.

Broderick shifted back to his human form. His underwear had torn off in his change to wolf and now he stood up, butt-naked—the butt in question too much in Mason's view.

"Thank you, sweetheart," Broderick said breathlessly.

Joanne smiled back at Mason's brother, very much in love with the dirtbag. The little protrusion in her belly was the obvious symbol of that love.

Aunt Cora, in a hot pink bathrobe with bunnies on it, popped around Joanne and took in the scene. "Thank the Goddess," she said. "I barely kept Aleck's mate from rushing in here. Mason, you all right? *Mason* … ?"

Mason felt himself shifting back to human whether he liked it or not. He lay against the wall, unable to move, his stomach raked open and gushing blood.

"Don't worry," he tried to say, but it came out all slurred. "I'm f—" The rest of the word faded, as did the room, and Mason slid into oblivion.

———

THE GOOD THING ABOUT HAVING A HALF-SHIFTER, half-Fae Lupine with healing powers in this Shiftertown was not only that she lived close by but also that she was gorgeous. Might be the painkiller talking, but Mason didn't mind looking his fill as Andrea Gray stitched up his wounds and sank her healing magic into him with the brush of her fingers.

So what if she was already mated to the Shiftertown's Guardian? Mason had no intention at all of touching the woman—she was a distant member of Mason's clan—but he could at least enjoy the beauty of her while she worked. Besides, she was Lupine, like him, plus she was the only thing in this house to enjoy right now.

For some reason, though Aleck had attacked,

everyone was pissed off at *Mason*. Aleck, finally waking from his tranqued state, had been calm again, his feral nature temporarily tucked away. He couldn't remember much, but he was pretty sure Mason had gone for him first, and Aleck had instinctively retaliated.

Mason, groggy from the painkillers Aunt Cora had given him, could only mumble in his defense. Nancy, Aleck's mate, had glared at Mason and asked why Mason couldn't accept that Aleck was ill and to leave him alone.

Goddess save me. Mason's room was a wreck, and there was no extra bedroom in this effing house for him to move into—no extra bed, period. He had to lie on the couch in the living room downstairs while Andrea sewed him up, which annoyed his three other brothers because they wanted to watch basketball.

Shifters had grown used to living in close quarters after being shoved into Shiftertowns, but this house was just getting stupid. Mason and his three brothers lived there with Aunt Cora, who kept them in line. Then Broderick had rescued Joanne's sister, Nancy, and had dragged home Aleck, a Feline pretty far gone into the feral state. Broderick had let them both live here, for fuck's sake, so that *his* mate, Joanne, who also lived here now, would be happy.

Someone should have put Aleck out of his misery a long time ago, in Mason's opinion. But then Nancy and her unborn cub would be grief-stricken, Joanne would be upset that her sister was unhappy, and Broderick would become even harder to live with than ever.

But what the hell were they going to do? Nancy would drop her cub any day, and Joanne was due in the fall. No one could predict what a feral Shifter would do to a tiny cub, even his own.

Ferals were Shifters who'd reverted into the wild things that lay at the core of every Shifter, the beast that reason deserted. The Shifter who started to slide into the feral state stopped bathing, forgot what forks were for, slept on the floor, and then just generally went foam-at-the-mouth crazy. Plus, ferals stank. The level of rank in this house had been going steadily up.

Most ferals either ran off into the wilderness to die of exposure, or they were killed by other Shifters to keep them from endangering the cubs. Aleck got to stay here and make their lives miserable while he hovered between sanity and the feral state. One day, though, they'd have to tranq him until he never woke up.

"Can't you do anything?" Mason asked Andrea as she sponged off his wound. "You're a healer. Fix him. Or at least make him smell better."

Andrea shook her head, dark hair moving in the spring breeze from the open windows. She was half Fae, which made her scent odd, but it was a hell of a lot better than feral Shifter. The draft blowing through the house didn't even make a dent in the stink from upstairs.

"I can heal wounds," Andrea said in her liquid voice. "Like yours." Light fingertips moved over Mason's stomach, the tingle of magic in them warming. "But Aleck is too far gone for me to reach, if I even knew how to reach him." Her brow furrowed in concern. "I'm not sure what we can do. Liam's called a meeting."

Liam was the Austin Shiftertown's leader. He was a Feline, but in spite of that drawback, he wasn't such a bad guy, even Mason had to admit. Liam decided what was good for Shiftertown and what to do about problems like Aleck.

"Liam's called a meeting for when?" Mason asked. "I'm going."

"It's starting now, but you're staying here." Andrea gave him a stern look.

"No." Mason pushed her warm hands away and struggled to his feet. His belly was a mess of lines and stitches, but Shifters healed quickly, and all this pain would go away soon. Right?

"Mason ..." Andrea's grip on his arm was surprisingly strong. "Broderick ..."

"Sit your ass down, Mason." Broderick loomed up from the dining room where they'd dragged the television. On it the Spurs were playing to rave enthusiasm from their human—and Shifter—fans. "I'm heading to Liam's meeting to tell him all about it."

"*Aleck's* version of the story," Mason said. He grabbed his T-shirt and eased it over his hurt stomach then carefully buttoned and buckled his jeans. "He's a fekking liar if he says I attacked him. I was *asleep* when that ton of Feline landed on me."

"Not a liar," Broderick said, trying to sound reasonable. "Ferals don't always know what's going on."

"Which is why we have to do something about him." Mason's voice turned to a snarl. Broderick was his alpha, but Mason couldn't hold back his defiance this time. Mason knew Broderick wasn't happy with the Aleck situation either, but his word was law in this house ... well, as long as Aunt Cora and Joanne didn't argue with him.

Broderick's eyes narrowed. "Mason, I'm taking care of it. Get back on that couch and heal up. Andrea, tranq him or something."

Andrea shook her head, put her torturing needle back into her bag along with the herbs she'd brought. "I'm not getting into a family fight, Broderick." She stood up and headed for the door without any apology.

"'Fraidy-cat," Mason called after her. The painkillers were making him a little woozy.

Andrea turned around and gave him a very wolf growl. "I'm mated to a Feline, and he's never afraid."

"No I meant … Never mind." Mason grabbed a motorcycle boot and tried to jam it on his foot. He realized it was Broderick's, kicked it off, and fished under the coffee table for his own.

By the time Mason got his boots on and made it to the front porch, Broderick was beside him. "I said I have this," Broderick growled.

"You're busy," Mason said, hanging on to the railing, the world spinning a little. "You've got a mate and a cub on the way and people to boss around. *I'm* the one who nearly got killed in the middle of the night. I'm going."

Broderick drew a sharp breath to say more, then he looked into Mason's eyes and stopped. Big brother observed him a while, always seeming to know what Mason was thinking. Then he gave a nod. "Fine. You can come with me. But keep quiet unless Liam asks you a direct question."

"I'm not afraid of Liam, the big bad Feline," Mason said, but that wasn't strictly true. Liam had a way of looking at a Shifter with quiet blue eyes and then putting him in his place without twitching a finger. Liam could be extraordinarily generous, and his mate and cub loved him to distraction, but there was no doubt that Liam ran the Austin Shiftertown with a firm paw.

The meeting took place at the bar just on the edge of Shiftertown, the bar not yet open for business. Liam was already there by the time Broderick and Mason walked in. He sat calmly on a barstool, one elbow resting on the bar behind him. Liam was manager here. Shifters weren't allowed to own businesses, so this bar belonged to a human, but there was no doubt that Liam actually ran it.

Sean, Liam's brother and Andrea's mate, walked in just behind Broderick and Mason, the Sword of the Guardian sticking up over Sean's shoulder. The sword unnerved Mason. A few months ago, Broderick had found a piece of another Guardian's sword, and the piece had not only burned a mark on Broderick's palm but sort of stuck with him like a lost puppy. It had done other weird things, and because of it, Mason, for a time, had thought his brother lost forever. He'd never told Broderick how empty and grief-stricken that had made him feel. Broderick's head was already big enough.

Liam was regarding Mason with his dark blue eyes as though he was trying to decide how culpable Mason was in Aleck's attack. Sean, with the same dark blue eyes as Liam, gave Mason a similar look. Mason only growled and slumped down into a chair. He still hurt, his mind fuzzy from the painkillers.

A few other Shifters were sitting here and there throughout the room. They were Liam's trackers—bodyguards, fighters, researchers—who generally helped Liam find trouble and keep the peace.

"Close the door," Liam said as soon as Broderick had gotten himself up on a barstool. The huge Kodiak bear Shifter, Ronan, who was the bar's bouncer, shut them in and locked the door.

"So then," Liam began in a calm voice. "It seems Aleck has become a bit of a problem."

"A *bit* of a problem?" Mason heard the snarl leave his

mouth before he could stop it. Must be the painkillers—he'd never have interrupted someone like Liam otherwise.

"A *bit*," Liam repeated firmly as Broderick tried to glare Mason to silence. "The poor lad's nearly gone, but he's got a mate and a cub on the way. If it comes down to finishing Aleck off, what becomes of his cub? Of Nancy?"

"Nancy's human," Mason said, still unable to keep his mouth shut. "She and Joanne have a family to take care of her."

"True," Liam conceded, "but what human family will want to raise a Shifter cub? They are a handful, to say the least." Liam shook his head but his look turned fond. He now had a baby Feline daughter who had him wrapped around her tiny fingers. "Nancy's sister is Broderick's mate, so your family, Mason, will have the keeping of Nancy and her cub, but the cub will be clanless."

The Shifters in the room moved restlessly in sympathy. A Shifter without a clan was in a precarious position —they had no natural protectors from the bad world or even from other Shifters. They'd be at the bottom of whatever pack or pride were kind enough to take them in, and finding a mate would be tough. Shifters had a taboo about breeding within their own clan, no matter how very distant the blood connection happened to be. If a Shifter's clan was unknown, other Shifters, especially of their own species, would be very reluctant to take them as mate.

Broderick shrugged as though none of this concerned him. "We can make the cub an honorary member of our clan and take care of him. Or her. That won't be a problem. Even though the cub will be a Feline."

He said *Feline* like an insult, and Liam, a Feline with a lot of lion in him, gave him a tiny smile.

"All right, so Nancy and the cub will have protectors," Liam went on. "But how do we tell the cub that we decided to kill his dad?"

Broderick returned Liam's look with a bland one of his own. "Easy. I'll send him to *you* when he's old enough and have you explain."

"Is killing him the only way?" Mason interrupted as Liam gave Broderick another of his tolerant smiles. "The guy sliced me open, yeah, but it's not his fault he's crazy. Can we just keep him seriously tranqued until he gets better?"

Sean was the one who answered. He shook his head. "From what Andrea and I have learned, the feral state eats into your brain—changes the chemistry and synapses. If we can't bring Aleck back soon, he'll have permanent brain damage. Then he'll be a danger not only to the Lupines he smells around him, but to his mate and even his own cub. We can't let that happen."

"So we off him?" Mason said. "Doesn't seem fair. Shifters have been brought back from the feral state before, right?"

Mason didn't know why he had this sudden rush of compassion for Aleck. The man had been raving and drooling more or less the whole time he'd lived in Mason's family home. In his few lucid periods, Aleck had been clear that he was grateful to them but didn't much like Lupines or any Collared Shifters at all. Dickhead. Must be Mason's painkillers making him soft.

Sean said, "If he's not too far gone, a healer could bring him back. *If* we can find a healer."

"Your mate," Mason said at once. "She healed *me*." He waved a hand at his abdomen, which still hurt, and met

Sean's gaze, his smart-ass mouth getting the better of him. "She has a fine touch."

Sean's eyes narrowed and a snarl left his throat. He went from concerned Guardian to possessive mate so fast that Mason laughed out loud.

"Peace," Liam rumbled, putting a calming hand on his brother's arm. "He's teasing you, Sean, and easy it is to do. No, lad, Andrea's a healer, but her gift comes from her Fae blood. Sean means a *Shifter* healer, one that's blessed by the Goddess with a strong amount of healing magic. A Shifter healer, it is said, can bring another Shifter back almost from the dead. They're powerful, rare, and extremely elusive. If I knew where I could get my hands on one, I would."

"That's it, then." Mason slapped the arms of his chair and pried himself to his feet. He swayed on those feet, still feeling the effects of his healing and the painkillers. "I'll go find us a Shifter healer, and we'll be done with this problem once and for all."

End of Excerpt

ALSO BY JENNIFER ASHLEY

Shifters Unbound

Pride Mates

Primal Bonds

Bodyguard

Wild Cat

Hard Mated

Mate Claimed

"Perfect Mate" (novella)

Lone Wolf

Tiger Magic

Feral Heat

Wild Wolf

Bear Attraction

Mate Bond

Lion Eyes

Bad Wolf

Wild Things

White Tiger

Guardian's Mate

Red Wolf

Midnight Wolf

Tiger Striped

A Shifter Christmas Carol

Shifter Made ("Prequel" short story)

Stormwalker

(w/a Allyson James)

Stormwalker

Firewalker

Shadow Walker

"Double Hexed"

Nightwalker

Dreamwalker

Dragon Bites

ABOUT THE AUTHOR

New York Times bestselling and award-winning author Jennifer Ashley has written more than 85 published novels and novellas in romance, urban fantasy, and mystery under the names Jennifer Ashley, Allyson James, and Ashley Gardner. Her books have been nominated for and won Romance Writers of America's RITA (given for the best romance novels and novellas of the year), several *RT BookReviews* Reviewers Choice awards (including Best Urban Fantasy, Best Historical Mystery, and Career Achievement in Historical Romance), and Prism awards for her paranormal romances. Jennifer's books have been translated into more than a dozen languages and have earned starred reviews in *Publisher's Weekly* and *Booklist*.

More about Jennifer's series can be found at http://www.jenniferashley.com.

CPSIA information can be obtained
at www.ICGtesting.com
Printed in the USA
BVHW041739210722
642702BV00014BA/174